Confessions of a Jackboy 3

Nicholas Lock

**Lock Down Publications & Ca$h
Presents
Confessions of a Jackboy 3
A Novel by *Nicholas Lock***

Lock Down Publications
P.O. Box 944
Stockbridge, Ga 30281

Visit our website at www.lockdownpublications.com

Book interior design by: **Shawn Walker**
Edited by: **Nuel Uyi**

Stay Connected with Us!

Text **LOCKDOWN** to 22828 to stay up-to-date with new releases, sneak peaks, contests and more…

Thank You.

Submission Guideline

Submit the first three chapters of your completed manuscript to ldpsubmissions@gmail.com, subject line: Your book's title. The manuscript must be in a .doc file and sent as an attachment. Document should be in Times New Roman, double spaced and in size 12 font. Also, provide your synopsis and full contact information. If sending multiple submissions, they must each be in a separate email.

Have a story but no way to send it electronically? You can still submit to LDP/Ca$h Presents. Send in the first three chapters, written or typed, of your completed manuscript to:

LDP: Submissions Dept
Po Box 944
Stockbridge, Ga 30281

*DO NOT send original manuscript. Must be a duplicate. *

Provide your synopsis and a cover letter containing your full contact information.

Thanks for considering LDP and Ca$h Presents.

Nicholas Lock

Chapter One

Corrigan had me fucked up! There was no way in the hell I was going to stick Ross! Did he know that me and Ross were homeboys? He had to be joking.

"Yea," Corrigan answered.

"One of these folders you gave me has Ross in it."

"I know. I pulled up on him and told him he had to pay a weekly tax of $20,000 and he laughed in my face. So, he needs to be taught a lesson. He thinks he's above the law!" Corrigan said to me.

"Look, Corrigan, that's one of my day ones right there. He needs a pass on the extortion tip."

"Last time I checked, he wasn't an Elite and you are, so all that is irrelevant. Your team of jackboys only get immunity because of the purpose they serve, but Ross isn't under our banner."

So, you're telling me to rob my nigga, a nigga that I have love for. A nigga that I've shed blood, sweat and tears for and with!" I said.

"That pretty much sums it up. Remember you're an Elite and nothing and no one comes above or before that," he reminded me but I didn't get that memo.

"Picture that," I hung up.

This was going to be a problem because I most definitely wasn't going to rob Ross. I just wondered how Corrigan was going to play it. I couldn't see the Elite tripping over something as minuscule as that. Robbing wasn't even their forte. We would just cross that bridge when they got to it, but it was a foregone conclusion that I wasn't robbing Ross.

"What's the business?" Ox asked. I had forgot he was even in the car.

7

"Nothing I can't handle but you need to pick another folder." I threw the folder with Ross in it on the back seat.

"I already did that." He showed me a different folder in his hand.

"I know I'm glad to be done with TNT though. They were starting to get under my skin plus I had my own issues I had to deal with."

"They can be overbearing sometimes," Ox laughed, "but their loyalty is unwavering."

"Yea, you right but, bro, I need to drop you off real quick. I need to handle something." I looked down at my phone.

"My nigga, you can drop me off anywhere and I'm good" he said, causing me to look over at him.

I wasn't going to leave my nigga out like that. I had enough time to get him right then dip off.

"Where you plan on staying at?" I inquired.

"I haven't given it any thought, to be real. To be honest, I'm still processing everything," Ox said, reaching in the ashtray and lighting the half blunt of sour diesel I had been smoking on earlier.

"I know the feeling, my G," I said, pulling the Porsche out of the county jail parking lot.

Our little duck-off spot across the river was empty because Murph had gotten a condo overlooking downtown and I had been moved out for the most part, so I was going to give it to Ox so he wouldn't have to worry about a place to lay his head at, and I was gonna lace my nigga's pockets with fifty racks. Besides, Trip's baby blue Mercedes wasn't doing anything but sitting around collecting dust, so why not give it to Ox! Ox's only worry would be whose daughter he was going to fuck tonight.

I pulled up to the split level and Ox asked:

"Whose spot is this?"

"Yours." I pulled the key off my key ring and gave it to him.

"Oh, word?" He grinned.

"The Benz is yours too," I said, getting out, walking up to the front door.

"This gon' have a nigga fucking all the hoes." Ox walked around the car, running his hand along the fender.

While Ox drooled over the Benz, I went inside to grab some money out of the safe. I had emptied it out for the most part. I just had a little bit of spending money inside. I went to my room, popped the safe open and took out fifty racks which left about twenty. I closed the safe door and came out the back as Ox walked in. I tossed him the money and dapped him up.

"I'm out, bro. I gotta handle this business. I'll hit you up later on."

I took off out the door and got in the Porsche, heading towards Ross's condo downtown. I had to find out exactly what had transpired between him and Corrigan and if could the situation be fixed, more than likely not.

I pulled into the condos off of Hay Street on Fountainhead Lane and made my way up to the second level.

"To what do I owe this pleasure?" Ross grinned, opening the door.

"I need to holler at you, my nigga" I walked past him into the lush condo.

This was my first time coming inside of the condo and had I known they were this exclusive, I would've bought one myself. Everything was top-of-the-line from the granite countertops to the marble floors. I took a seat at the breakfast bar as Ross grabbed us two bottles of *Dr. Pepper*.

"Now what the hell are you doing here at 4 o'clock in the morning?" He sat down beside me.

"Did a detective pull up on you on some crazy shit?"

"Hell yea. Nigga told me I had to pay a weekly tax and he would allow me to keep doing my thang. Ha! I told him to go fuck himself." Ross threw his hand as if waving the statement off. "Wait. How do you know about that?"

"Because that detective is how I get the drop on all the D-boys I be hitting. But look, bro, throwing him some crumbs every week is a beneficial move to all parties involved," I said and Ross shook his head.

"Face, if I didn't know any better, I would think you're telling me to agree to being extorted." Ross narrowed his eyes.

"No. What I'm telling you to do is, be smart and use the brain God gave you. No matter your decision, my nigga, you know I'm riding regardless but check it out. If a street nigga had approached you about paying, you know I'd say stretch that nigga ass out. But this is the head Narc in the city—"

"I could give two fucks! I don't care if he was the head Narc in the world!" Ross snapped, cutting me off

"What are you out here yelling about?" Diqueena walked out the back in a black lingerie set. "Oh my God. Hey, Face!" She ran over and gave me a hug.

"Go put some clothes on," Ross told her and she waved him off.

"Boy, Face is like my brother and he's seen me naked plenty of times," Diqueena said.

"Go put some clothes on, Diqueena," I said, seeing the look on Ross's face.

She rolled her eyes and walked into the back

"Bra, look—" I started to say, but Ross cut me off again.

"If you're about to say something about that police then I don't want to hear it"

"Say no more, my nigga, if this is how you want to play it then that's what it is. I'm with it but I am gonna say this— you're doing something wrong." I threw the folder on the bar.

"Look at everything he knows," I continued as Ross looked over the folder.

"Remember a chain is only as strong as its weakest link," I reminded him and left him to check the folder out in its entirety.

Nicholas Lock

Chapter Two

I was at *Pleasure's* in my office going over some paperwork when Lauren walked in looking like something out of a *Straight Stuntin* magazine.

"What it do, Lauren?"

"Game time," she said seriously

"What are you talking 'bout, woman?"

"You want Diablo out of your hair—well, phase one of getting rid of him starts tonight. He's getting a big shipment of black tar tonight!" Lauren said.

Diablo was part of the Sinaloa Cartel. He was actually the one who was rumored to be about to take El Chapo's position with him locked up. Me, Wolf, and Murph had hit him for some bricks of heroin with the help of TNT. Since then, he'd killed some members of TNT and sent me a message that I needed to return the work or else! I had yet to find out how he had even found out it was us. But Lauren's plug—Chino— was also in the Sinaloa Cartel, and he wanted Diablo out of the way so he could be the next one to head the cartel. He was going to help me get rid of Diablo.

"Just tell me the location and he'll never get it!" I vowed.

"There's going to be an eighteen-wheeler parked behind the Walmart in Spring Lake tonight—you know what to do," she said suggestively.

I nodded, thinking of who I was going to take with me because this sting was important. If I got my hands on Diablo's re-up, it would give me a leg up. No matter who you are, it costs to go to war and if your main source of income got cut off, it would affect you in a major way.

"Penny for your thoughts." Lauren strutted her way around my desk and hopped up on it.

"You comfortable?" I looked at her thick thighs coming out from under the purple Fendi mini she had on.

"I am now." She lifted one of the white stilettos she had on and rested it on the arm of my chair, giving me a clear view up her mini.

"Lauren, you're not gonna be satisfied until I fuck the shit out of you." I continued to stare up her mini at her shaved pussy.

"You're right." Lauren got up and straddled my lap. "Nigga, me and you together would look so good." She tried to unbuckle my belt.

Me and Lauren had gotten super cool since I had found out she was Ross's plug. It was nothing to see me and her out having drinks or just kicking it. The sexual tension was super thick between us but I would never act on it. Lauren and her little sister had a body that was created to provide sexual pleasure. She was 5'11, 180 pounds with DD's and what I could only guess was a fifty-inch ass that was all natural. Then she had the nerve to have some real chinky eyes and naturally long lashes, giving her an exotic look. I couldn't cap, her mocha complexion looked good as hell.

"Nah, ma, we can't do that. I ain't trying to complicate things between us, plus I got a bitch." I tried to move her off my lap.

"Ain't nobody gon' know. You just gon' be my friend friend." She got up, turned around and lifted her mini up over her ass.

Lauren looked back over her shoulder while grabbing the desk and said, "You scared of this pussy."

I dropped my pants, put a Trojan on and slid inside Lauren's dripping wet love box. I fucked her for the next hour. When we got done, she said: "You know this is only the beginning."

***

"Why don't we just go over there and check it out?" Tatianna's dark, super thick ass inquired.

I had decided to take Rai'chell and her all-girl crew to take the eighteen-wheeler down.

"Patience, girl, patience," Chell said softly.

It was me, Chell, Jasmine's ugly yellow bone ass, Sidney and her brown-skinned, thick self with her pretty green eyes, Marquita's redbone petite ass and Tatianna's dark chocolate thick impatient ass.

To be completely honest, Chell and her crew were more ruthless than the niggas in JBM. They used to shoot niggas in the ass after they robbed them but I had told them that was really stupid. If you were going to let your pistol bark, you might as well go ahead and kill them and that's what they started doing much to the chagrin of Corrigan. I asked them why they were shooting niggas in the ass and they said it was payback for all the niggas that had done them wrong. We were sitting in a Dodge Caravan watching the eighteen-wheeler. I was hoping Diablo was going to show his face so I could put a few hollow points in it but I knew the chances of that were slim to none.

"There's a truck pulling up," Sidney pointed.

I looked as a gray F-150 pulled up beside the eighteen-wheeler and four Mexicans got out, none of them Diablo. One of them opened the back of the eighteen-wheeler, and that was our cue. Marquita gunned the engine, causing the caravan to jump in the direction of the eighteen-wheeler. Rai'chell slid the side door open and the girls started letting their hammers spit. The Mexicans were dead before they knew what hit them. We all hopped out to see what was in the back.

"Holy shit!" Sidney gasped.

The back of the eighteen-wheeler was filled with bricks! Way too many to unload into the van.

"Quita, can you drive this big motherfucker?" Jasmine questioned.

Marquita weighed the question before nodding by way of saying, *yes*. Marquita was the designated driver of the group, and she was all the way like that behind the wheel.

"Well, let's go then!" Chell said with conviction.

"Sidney, you ride with Quita and here—" I passed her my M16.

Sidney was the shooter out of the group. All of them were shooters but Sidney didn't know what it meant to hesitate.

"We're going to Taylor's Creek and we're gonna follow you," said Chell.

Marquita got behind the wheel of the eighteen-wheeler, crunk it up and took off with us behind her.

"Bro, I'm on the way to Taylor Creek with so much work it really don't make no sense. I told you I was gonna make you the king of the city. Well, here it is!" I told Ross and hung up.

We got to Taylor Creek without incident. Ross had four vans waiting on us when we got there.

"Hold up, bro, we need to count them first so we can know how many it is because they're not free." Jasmine glared at him.

"You got it," Ross put his hands up in surrender.

They opened the back up and got in.

"Face, it's money in here too," Tatianna said.

"Look, get them birds out of there and we'll get to the money in a minute," I urged them.

I didn't like being around all them bricks because I knew for a fact that they were life sentences. There had to be at least three to four hundred bricks of black tar heroin in the eighteen wheeler. I'd rather get locked up for a murder charge; at least

I knew I had a chance at beating it, but if the jokes pulled up right now it would be an open-and-shut case. They loaded all four vans up and, as I had guessed, there were three hundred and fifty bricks.

"Look, bro, we need four million apiece. Me and Chell can wait but you need to straighten the other girls," I said.

"Don't act like you not super straight, nigga, because you're the only one in the entire city with black tar," Chell added.

"And we're the reason you don't have any competition," Sidney chimed in.

"Give me a few days and I'll have y'all straight," Ross said sincerely.

"Don't make us come looking for you." Marquita looked my nigga in the eyes.

Ross left with the vans, leaving us with the eighteen wheeler. We unloaded the cash and took it to Jasmine's spot. It only added up to three mil. I let them split the bread amongst themselves and they went crazy. Me and Chell left together. I needed to spend some time with her and my son before she got back on her bullshit.

Nicholas Lock

Chapter Three

"Face, I stumbled up on some shit that will make our lives easier when it comes to this jackboy shit," Maino told me.

"A'ight, where you at?" I questioned while loading my .40.

"In Harnett County."

"Give me the address and I'll be there in about thirty minutes."

"Where you about to go?" Angie asked, washing the dishes from the breakfast she had cooked for me.

"You mean where we about to go," I stated and she ran in the back to get dressed, leaving the dishes unfinished. I laughed and finished loading my hammer. I had been spending more time with Angie since her revelation about being pregnant. I had yet to tell Chell about Angie being pregnant because we had finally got back to a good place in our relationship, and news about Angie being pregnant might shatter it. So I was waiting on the right time. So if there was such a thing, I wonder what Maino had ran across that had him talking like that because shit was already easy if you ask me. Since I had put Maino in charge of Jackboy Mafia, there hadn't been not one setback or hiccup, so I had to trust his judgment. Then with Rai'chell and her crew of Jack girls putting in work, I didn't see why my plan of owning all the high-end clubs wouldn't come to fruition within the next year. Then once I was able to hit Alvaro, that would set the standard. To rob the head of the Medellin Cartel would put me in a position like no other and give me a god-like status. You don't hear about cartel leaders getting robbed, at least not in the U.S. but I was determined to fix that. Yea, Chief and Alvaro Calderon were going to be my last stings. After them, I was going to hang up my ski mask and focus on being the King of the night life on the east coast one city at a time. And once the Diablo beef gets put to rest, my only worry is going to be how I'm going to spend all my money. Angie came back out the back as I was putting my gun on my waist. I looked up at her and asked: "Where you about to go?"

"What you mean?" I thought I was going with you." Angie started looking crazy.

I think she was just fucking with me.

"Angie, stop fucking playing with me. You know I'm not taking you with me and you got them little ass shorts on."

She had changed to some orange boy shorts that had the bottom of her ass out and a white t-shirt.

"Ain't nothing wrong with my shorts," she grinned and walked over to me. "What? I don't look good in these?" Angie wrapped her arms around my neck.

"Angie, we're about to go around a bunch of dudes you don't know for a quick minute or two, so what would I look like bringing my bitch around with her ass hanging out?" I looked her in the eyes.

"I didn't know, baby." She cast her eyes down and went to change.

While she went to change, I went and got in the Porsche. Kevin Gates' "Big Gangsta" blared out the alpines as I waited for Angie to come out. I was about to leave her ass when she came out wearing a pink Prada short set and some white and pink 4's.

"Cute, right?" Angie smiled.

I just looked at her. It was no denying the fact that I had major love for her. Angie hooked her phone up to the radio and put on Summer Walker's album. I shook my head and pulled off. Angie reached over, grabbed my hand and laced her hand into mine.

"You know I love your sexy ass," Angie squeezed my hand.

"Sometimes," I grinned, causing her to smack her lips.

Angie tried to take her hand out of mine but I wouldn't let go.

"Girl, you know I know you love me, stop pouting with your spoiled ass." I leaned over and kissed her cheek.

We talked about our future and baby names the rest of the ride to Harnett County. I followed the GPS to the outskirts to a city called Dunn.

"Oh, hell no!" I said when I saw that I was supposed to drive down an uneven dirt road.

I called Maino.

"Man, why you ain't tell me I had to drive down a dirt road?" I asked. "I'm in the Porsche," I added.

'That's your problem. Ain't nobody tell your ass to drive that death trap," Maino said.

"You a mock!" I said.

He started laughing. "I'm about to send somebody up there."

"So what are we going to do?" Angie asked after I hung up.

"They're about to send somebody to get us."

About five minutes later Abdullah and G'd-up rode up on two dirt bikes. For what reason I didn't know.

"What's good?" they both asked when I stepped out of the car.

"Niggas like us," I dapped both of them up. "Where the car at?"

"You looking at them," G'd up grinned.

"You gotta ride, bitch," Abdullah laughed but I didn't.

Angie stepped out of the Porsche and I said to Abdullah, "It looks like you gotta ride bitch now."

He shook his head and got off the bike. I got on with Angie behind me and Abdullah on the back of G'd up's bike. I followed them down the dirt road until we got to where everyone was at. When I saw the entire JBM together, all I could do was shake my head. The first person I locked eyes with was Chell. Then when Angie got off the back of the dirt bike with her baby bump, Chell's eyes narrowed to slits.

"Took your ass long enough," Streets said with an easy smile.

"He was too good to drive his little foreign car down the dirt road," Maino flashed a grin.

"Damn right!" I said.

"Hey, baby daddy!" Chell walked up to me, wrapped her arms around my neck and stuck her tongue in my mouth.

"What up?" I said softly.

"Us. Hey, Angie! Let me find out you done let one of them doctors pop a baby in you." Chell looked down at Angie's stomach.

"Girl, no" Angie turned red.

"Okay, let's get to the reason we're here," Maino cut in.

"This shit gon' blow your mind, bo," Ratchet said.

"Fact!" Marquita's pretty redbone ass chimed in.

I couldn't cap, every member of Jackboy Mafia fit the mold for what I had envisioned, I thought to myself as I looked them over. Chell and her crew of Jack girls were the icing on the cake. They gave the Jackboy Mafia an added element. They could get in places and at niggas that we normally couldn't.

"Come on," Maino led the way. Chell tried to hold my hand as we started walking but I stopped that right away. "You know this ain't personal time. We're here on business," I said to her.

Everyone knew Chell was my girl but while we were on our robbing shit, I wanted to keep things businesslike. I was their leader and I didn't want them to get the impression that I wasn't on my shit. Plus I had Angie with me. I put my arm on Angie's shoulder as we walked. I had Chell on my left and Angie on my right. It was crazy because Angie knew what was up with Chell and me, but all Chell knew about me and Angie was that we had a super strong bond.

We followed Maino around a bend and came upon some kind of obstacle course and some buildings. The next thing I saw were three big German Shepherds running our way barking. Everyone pulled their guns but before any of us could squeeze, an older white man yelled: "Stop!" The dogs stopped on a dime. Maino greeted the man with a handshake.

"Fred, these are my people. Y'all, this is Fred. He used to train all the SWAT teams and K-9's in the surrounding areas." Maino introduced us.

"K-9's?" Sidney focused her green eyes on the dogs.

"Yea, K-9's," Maino said. "Drug-sniffing K-9's."

"Word!" Snub said, swinging his shoulder-length dreads.

Chapter Four

It was all starting to make sense. We were already killing the game but if we could get our hands on dogs that could sniff out work, that would put us head and shoulders above the game. Unstoppable was the word that came to mind.

In the end, we left with two K-9's, and Fred was going to train JBM how to hit houses like a SWAT team.

"You thought they got active with you but they get re-tarded active with me," Ox bragged.

"We're about to find out in a little bit, ain't we?" I said.

"He's talking that big boy talk, ain't he?" Murph asked, sitting on the couch in my office at *Pleasure's Paradise*.

Me, Murph, Ox, and TNT were getting ready to run down on Jake, the owner of *Club Aqua*. I had sent Chell to tell him to sign the club over to me. I was going to give him a million in cash. Instead of him agreeing, he cursed Chell out and had her escorted out of the club, so I was taking this one personal.

"What the hell are y'all doing? Let's get to this action!" Chell said the instant she barged into my office.

"Goddamn! You too pretty to be getting active, come sit on my lap and let me be the one to get dirty," Ox told Chell, not knowing any better.

"Nigga, do you know who I am?" She looked at me and I raised a brow.

"Yeah, my soon-to-be woman," Ox grinned.

"Face is my husband," she said, causing Ox to look my way.

"Why you didn't say shit, bro?" asked Ox.

"She can handle herself as you can see.

"Man, let's go!" Chell was anxious to get back at Jake.

We all filed out of my office and ran into Pocahontas.

"I need to talk to you," she grabbed my arm, causing Chell to look at her like she had two heads.

"I'll holler at you when I get back." I tried to keep going but she had a firm grip on my arm.

"There's a Mexican at the bar that says he needs to talk to you right now or he's going to turn the club into a crime scene."

We all broke into a run trying to see if it was who we thought it was and, sure enough, Diablo was at the bar casually drinking a beer. My first instinct was to stretch him but to do so in my club would be a bad look. Then Diablo was way too comfortable, knowing he was behind enemy lines. I took in Diablo's stature as I walked up to the bar. Diablo was about my height which was 6'0, slim, with long black hair, a prominent nose and small beady eyes. He turned our way as we walked up to him.

"You have a serious death wish!" I glared at Diablo.

"Says the man who robbed the Sinaloa Cartel!" he shot back.

"Fuck you and the cartel!" Ox snapped.

"You talk tough but me not believe it," he said and spit on the floor by Ox's feet. I had to hold Ox back from going in Diablo's shit.

"It's a lot of unnecessary talking going on. Either he's going to die in this club or not," Chell spoke.

"Stay in your place, bitch!" he spat. Before I could get to him Chell rushed over and put a pink .380 under Diablo's chin, causing him to smile, revealing black rotten teeth.

"Chill, Chell," I said and she backed away. Diablo laughed.

"There are five hundred ese's outside right now waiting for my signal—without it, everyone inside is to be killed. You have seventy-two hours to return my bricks or you and everyone close to you die."

I looked at Ox and he got on the phone to call TNT who was also outside waiting on us.

I knew Ox had to have something up his sleeve and now I knew what it was. Ox got off the phone and nodded, letting me know he wasn't him.

"You're not in Mexico anymore, so your threats carry little weight here," Murph warned.

I was in a Catch-22. I felt like I was damned if I did and damned if I didn't. Fuck it, I was thuggin!

"Snatch him up," I said, then Murph and Ox grabbed Diablo up and took him to the back. No one batted an eye because it wasn't uncommon to see someone getting carried out the club.

"Diablo, you thought the power you have in Mexico was going to transfer to my city but you were sadly mistaken, and it's going to cost you your life," I said to him when we got back to my office.

"To kill me is to kill your family," Diablo continued to make threats.

"Ox, go out there and show them how we give it up in the city."

While Ox went outside to team up with TNT to give it to the Mexicans, Murph and Chell tied Diablo's hands behind his back.

I grabbed the trashcan and walked behind Diablo.

"Thank Chino," I said and wrapped the bag around his head.

Diablo tried to wiggle out from under me but that only caused me to tighten my grip on the bag, further cutting off Diablo's air supply. Diablo lost his bowels and his life. I looked over at the camera monitors and saw Lauren standing between Ox, TNT, and all the Mexicans. I, Chell and Murph rushed outside to see what she had going on. As we got outside, one of the Tiaras tried to sneak Lauren but Lauren ducked and came up with a right hook that knocked her out cold.

"Chill!" I stepped in front of Lauren as TNT attempted to rush her.

"Fuck that!"

"Face, you sent me out here to give these spics the business and this bitch not only interfered but she put her hands on one of mine." Ox's voice betrayed his frustration.

Before I could say anything, Lauren spoke up.

"If you would've listened, you would know that they mean you no harm. They're under Chino's command now and since Diablo didn't come back out, I'm assuming he's dead.

I could see the blood lust in Ox's and TNT's eyes.

"We still gon' fuck up Club Aqua, my G, just chill," I reassured him.

"Chino wants to speak with you," Lauren informed me. On cue, a red Denali pulled up; they went rigid. They all moved in around the Denali. The back window rolled down, revealing a chubby Mexican with a neck full of thick Cuban links and a sneering Karla.

"Chino, this is Face. Face, this is Chino." Lauren made the introduction.

"What's the deal?" Chino asked me in flawless English and stuck his fist out for a pound.

"I can't call it, my G." I bumped his fist with mine, causing him to smile, showing me he had a mouth full of gold which caught me off guard. Chino reminded me of the Mexicans that grew up in the hood around the city; he had black mannerism. I could tell by looking at him that he had a little bit of age on him. I guessed him to be in his mid-to-late 30's.

"You did me a major favor by dealing with Diablo. How-ever way I can help you, let me know?" he asked and Karla rolled her eyes.

I was going to have Lauren holler at her sister because she obviously had some animosity towards me. I turned Chino's question over in my head. See, Chino was a snake because he went against his own to improve his position and if he did his own people like that, then he wouldn't think twice about smoking me. But I knew someone in his position that could help me in ways unimaginable.

"You know what, Chino? You can help me. As you can see, I have a team that needs to be fed." I swept my head around, showing him TNT. "I know you distribute work to a lot of people that I'm more than sure you don't particularly care for. Allow me to rob them and I'll give you the work back. That way, you'll still be winning." I knew I had to throw him a bone.

Chino took no time mulling over what I said

"Deal. I'll give Lauren the information as it comes," he said and rode off.

I turned to Ox and I could see him and TNT still wanted action.

"Y'all wanna get active, come on. I'll catch up to you later on, Lauren."

I was about to let them take their frustrations out on *Club Aqua* and its owner.

Nicholas Lock

Chapter Five

"Who is Lauren to you?" Chell asked from the passenger seat, causing Murph to laugh.

I glared at him in the backseat through the rearview mirror because his laugh was going to cause Chell to get on her bullshit. And I didn't need any distractions at the moment.

"Nobody, really," I said, trying to leave it at that.

"What you mean *really*?" She turned to face me

"We'll talk about it after we leave *Club Aqua*." I was starting to get mad.

"No, we about to talk about it right now!" she shrieked.

"Since you're the reason she on this dumb shit, you tell her who the fuck Lauren is."

Seeing shit was about to get crazy for real, Murph went ahead and gave Chell the rundown on Lauren and her sister.

"Oh, so you saving bitches now!"

"It obviously paid off but check this, Rai'chell, she ain't nobody to me and that's my last time saying it. Ask me again and you gon' get the fuck out and walk."

Chell sat back in the seat fuming but didn't say nothing else; she knew I was dead serious now.

We pulled into *Club Aqua* and parked. I looked around and saw Jake's black Mercedes parked in the front, letting me know he was inside. We had paid the bouncer previously so we all got in the club with our pistols. Everyone fanned out, with Chell and Murph staying with me. I looked around the club and was impressed. *Club Aqua* was about nine thousand square feet and held close to five thousand people. The club had a nice vibe to it, there were all types of people walking around. I initially thought *Club Aqua* was a hood club but I was mistaken. The blue and white color scheme gave off a cool, relaxed atmosphere. I looked towards the VIP section and saw a group of white boys standing on the white couches turning up while Jack Harlow's new joint bumped throughout the club. I had to change my initial plan of burning the club down; there was too much money at stake. While I was taking everything in, a bouncer came up to Chell and grabbed her arm.

"Didn't Jake tell you not to come inside here again?" She shook her head at me before I could reach.

"Take me to him. I need to speak with him," Chell told the bouncer.

He doesn't want to talk to you now, let's go!" he said, jerking her arm.

Chell jerked her arm back and slid up close to him, putting her gun to his side and said, "But I want to talk to him, now move."

He looked to me and Murph with a look, like, *Help me,* then I said harshly: "You heard what the fuck she said, now move!"

The bouncer led us to the back where Jake's office was. Chell pushed him through the door and he fell on the floor of the office.

"What the hell!" Jake stood up.

"Sit your pussy ass down before I put a slug in your head!" Murph warned.

Jake had a white dude in his office sitting down; he looked familiar but I wasn't able to place his face at first then it hit me.

"Well, well, well. Mr. Darrell, I've been trying to run you down for the longest." I grinned.

Darrell was the owner of five clubs in the city. And I wanted all of them but there were two in particular that were a must have. One was a gentlemen's club called *Bottoms Up.*

Anytime you passed by, the parking lot would be full of luxury cars. They mainly catered to doctors, lawyers, and other high-paying jobs. The other one was called *The Ranch;* it was a nightclub that was packed every single night. It wasn't a hip hop club; it was a pop club. *The Ranch* always had big name pop stars coming through. Taylor Swift had just come a few days ago. If I could get all of Darrell's clubs, I would be the owner of every high-end club and strip club in the city.

"I don't think we've ever met," Darrell said, looking me in my face as if he would recognize me.

"We haven't but today is your unlucky day. Jake, I'm sure by now you know why we're here. Maybe you can inform Mr. Darrell here why it is we're in your office," I said with a smirk.

"These hooligans think they can get us to sign our clubs over to them with idle threats," Jake said, picking his cellphone up.

Before he could dial a number, Chell rushed around the desk and took the phone right out of his hand. Jake tried to stand up but Chell pushed him back in his chair and put a butterfly knife through his right hand and into his desk.

"Holy shit!" Darrell yelled, standing up, knocking over the chair he was sitting in.

"It's only a little blood, Darrell." Murph grinned and sat Darrell back in his chair.

I looked at Jake sweating bullets, gritting his teeth and looking down at his hand that was nailed to his cherry wood desk.

"What he didn't tell you was that I offered to give him a million dollars for the club," I informed Darrell.

"I make that in two and a half months with my club," Jake said through gritted teeth.

"Look, fellas, I don't want any trouble. I was here selling him—"

"Shut up!" Jake cut Darrell off. "Aaahh!" he yelled because Chell twisted the knife in his hand.

"What were you about to say?" Murph questioned.

"I was about to sell Jake all of my clubs for four point five million."

"Sold! Where's the paperwork?" I asked urgently.

Darrell pointed at the desk; the papers had blood on them. But I could care less. Me and Darrell both signed the papers, making me the owner of all five of his clubs. Darrell walked out of the office four and a half million dollars richer but most importantly he left with his life.

"What are you gon' do, homey?" Murph was ready to leave.

"I'm not giving you anything! I'll die before I sign my club over" Jake glared at us.

Boom! Boom! Chell put two bullets through his chest, knocking him out of his chair onto his back. I peeked over the desk just as Jake's eyes glossed over. We walked out of the office and I nodded at Ox, giving him the sign to go ahead and cut up.

"Tali! Tali! Tali!" TNT started chanting as me, Murph, and Chell walked out the club.

There was no need for us to stay and watch them cut up. I got what I needed to get done *done*. Then with Jake dead and a mini massacre at *Club Aqua,* City Council was going to shut the club down. Then I would be able to come buy the lease, change the name and open the club back up. So, I was going to win regardless; I was officially the king of the nightlife in Fayetteville!

Chapter Six

"Why haven't you robbed Ross yet?" Corrigan asked me.

All of the Elite were in attendance at the Weeks' house. We had just gotten done discussing how we were going to welcome the head of the Elite into town. I hadn't seen Ryan Bush since I was made a member.

"Because I'm not," I said with conviction.

"You realize what you're saying?" Corrigan asked, his face darkening

"What's going on?" Special Agent Liu inquired, sensing the tension in the room.

"Face seems to think he can go against the Elite," Corrigan said, causing the entire room to look my way.

"What is he talking about?" Billy, the de facto leader, asked me.

"A whole bunch of nothing. Corrigan wants me to rob one of my day ones. Someone I have genuine love for. A person that I consider family." I looked everyone in the eyes as I spoke.

"He isn't an Elite, so he doesn't matter!" Corrigan said

"Consuela, does your daughter matter even though she's not an Elite?" I questioned the district attorney.

"Of course," she said immediately

"He's not your family, dammit!" Corrigan slammed his fist down on the table.

"Corrigan, calm down, it's not that serious," Tasha chimed in

"Either you rob him or I'm gonna lock him up forever!" Corrigan warned, causing me to look back his way.

"Lock him up and I'm gon' put so many holes in you the devil is gonna feel sorry for you!" I shot back.

"You see! He has no respect for the Elite!" he protested.

"You can't threaten him, Face," Mark, the Chief of Police, said softly.

I looked around the round table and it just dawned on me that I really didn't belong. I was the only street nigga in the room. I was in a room with the mayor, a federal prosecutor, an F.B.I. agent, a D.E.A agent, the sheriff, the chief of police, a judge, a D.A, a lawyer, another judge, and a surgeon. The only reason I initially joined was because of the resources and the doors they could open. Not to mention they controlled the legal system all over. I really didn't need them; shit, I was up! They needed me and my team. The only people in the room I had love for was Cynthia's mom and dad; everyone else could die slow.

"You know what? Fuck all this. I'm outta here!" I got up and walked out the house

I had bigger fish to fry. I needed to focus on how I was going to rob Chief.

"Bro, where you at?" I called Wolf.

"At Pocahontas' spot."

"I'm about to come through," I told him and hung up.

I pulled into Pocahontas' condo and parked. Hopefully, she wasn't here because I needed to talk to my young boy about hitting her brother, Chief. Chief ran the entire Robeson County which was the biggest county in North Carolina, land wise, and there was about thirty small cities inside of Robeson County. Chief supplied his people with high grade coke and heroin. He was the first person I had ever seen with a Rolls-Royce. Chief had been above the game for the longest, so his pockets were deep as the Atlantic Ocean. If we were able to rob Chief, we would have to keep it from Pocahontas. He was her bread and butter. And you could tell by the way she talked about him that she loved him to no end.

"What up, big bro?" Wolf dapped me up when he opened the door.

"Damn!" I said, walking into the condo and seeing all the ass running around.

Pocahontas had a bunch of her homegirls at her place and all they had on was bra and panties.

"Hey, Face!" Danielle strutted over and hugged me

"Sup, Brown Sugar?" I used her stage name.

"This D," she grabbed my dick through my jeans I moved her hand and shook my head

"Come on, bro, before she rape you," Wolf joked.

"You can't rape the willing!" Brown Sugar yelled at our back.

We walked out to the balcony and closed the door.

"Your young ass be in heaven around all this pussy." I smirked

"Big facts!" Wolf smiled, looking out over the city.

Wolf was only sixteen but my boy got super active! And he was a white boy with plaits down his back. He was a part of TNT but I had taken him under my wing and was giving him the game. The thing I liked the most, besides his gun play, was the fact that he could think.

"What have you found out about Chief?"

"Just about everything. Pocahontas get tipsy and be running off at the mouth. I know where he stay, where his side bitch stay, two of his stash spots and I know he go to Kickback Jacks every Thursday," he said smugly.

"Okay then!" We about to take him out the game."

"What are y'all out here doing?" Pocahontas walked her pretty ass out onto the balcony in a thong and bra followed by Brown Sugar smoking a blunt. "Curiosity killed the cat," I said.

"Boy Boo!" Pocahontas waved me off and wrapped her arms around Wolf.

"Let me hit that," I said to Brown Sugar and she shook her head by way of saying, *No.*

Brown Sugar was standing in the doorway in some gray see-through boy shorts and a see-through black bra. She had her legs locked back poking her bubble butt out. Brown Sugar was 5'0, 165 pounds, with soft brown eyes and a smooth pecan brown skin tone. Then she had natural honey blond hair that fell to the middle of her back and she was pigeon toed. Which made her pussy poke out in all.

Baby girl was like that!

"Damn! You sweating my girl, ain't you?" Pocahontas put me on the spot.

"I'm sweating that fat ass blunt she blowing on," I lied, leaning up against the railing.

"Whining ass nigga!" Brown Sugar said, walking between my legs and putting the blunt in my mouth.

I pulled on the blunt and instantly exhaled. I passed Wolf the blunt, and Brown Sugar grabbed both of my hands and put them on her ass. Her shit was dumb soft. I felt my dick stretching out in the Amiri jeans I was wearing. She rubbed her knee on my wood and pulled me to her until we were face to face.

"Come fuck this pussy," she said softly, staring me in the eyes."

"Next time," I said, breaking free from her grasp. "Wolf, call me tomorrow," I said and walked out.

I had to go home to Chell. There's no way I was going home smelling like pussy!

Chapter Seven

I pulled onto Angie's street and saw a line of cars parked by her house.

"What you got going on at our house?" I called and asked her as I sat at the stop sign down the road from her house.

"Hey, babe! My brother and dad are in town and they stopped to check on me. Come on, I want you to meet them.

"Okay, I'm about to pull up."

The closer I got to Angie's house, I saw a bunch of men standing in and around her yard.

"They brought the whole family with them," I said out loud as I pulled into her yard.

Something wasn't right, I thought, taking the men in.

Their posture and body language was tense and then I saw the earpieces. What the fuck! I grabbed and cocked my Glock .29 and got out. The minute I got out of my car, they all focused on me. They were playing! If any one of them made the wrong move, I was gon' up my fire, no questions asked. I'd figure everything out after the smoke cleared; a few of them nodded while the rest watched as I walked up to the house. I walked into the house and got the surprise of my life! In Angie's living room sat Alvaro Calderon, the head of the Medellin cartel.

"Face!" Angie walked up to me and kissed me on the lips. This is my brother Domonick and my dad," she introduced us.

I had a bewildered look on my face.

They looked absolutely nothing alike. Where Angie had a deep caramel color, they were a white looking pale color.

"Nice to meet you, Domonick and Mister—?" I shook both of their hands.

"Just call me Al," he said, looking me up and down.

I could tell he didn't approve but I could care less. If I had things my way, he would be a dead man in the coming weeks.

"Anyway, we got to get moving but I'm going to send a car for you later tonight so you can come by the house. Make sure you go home shopping and let me know what you find. So I can call the banker and get the paperwork done. I'll be seeing you around, young man," he said and left, followed by his son.

"That didn't go the way I planned," Angie nibbled on her bottom lip.

"Why is that?" I grabbed Angie up and carried her pregnant ass to the bedroom.

"I just expected it to go differently, that's all," she said once I sat her on the bed and laid down.

"That isn't your real dad or brother," I said to her.

"What makes you say that?" Angie questioned, laying down beside me, resting her head on my chest.

"You don't have any of their features, not one." I ran my hand along her body.

"You're right, they're not my real dad and brother, but they somewhat like it," said Angie.

"Somewhat like it, huh? Your play daddy is the head of one of the most notorious and ruthless cartels in the world." I let her know that I knew who he was. Angie popped her head up off my chest and looked at me.

"Yea, I know who he is but I want to know who he really is to you."

"Okay, listen, you already know that I'm really from Cuba. See, when I was young, Alvaro came to Cuba to do some business and it was there that he met my mother. They said it was love at first sight. He married my mother six months later. And moved us to Columbia. Only Domonick was two years older than me, so we immediately clicked. I was only ten at the time. I got spoiled rotten. I was the only little girl in Columbia with a Cabbage Patch doll. This was the eighties. Everything was perfect but then when I was fourteen. Me and my mom were downtown shopping when one of Alvaro's rivals kidnapped us and held us for ransom. They held us for three days. During those three days they repeatedly had their way with my mom, then once the ransom was paid, they drove us downtown and threw us on the street. Right before they pulled off, they shot my mom in the face at point blank range." Angie started to cry.

"It's okay, baby girl." I tried to hold her but she pushed me away.

"Let me finish," Angie croaked. "Things weren't the same after that. I blamed Alvaro for my mother's death. If he would've left us in Cuba, my mother would still be alive. I started rebelling and he sent me to school over here where I got my nursing license. I completely cut off all lines of communication between us. Today was my first time seeing or hearing from them in about twenty years," she confessed.

I grabbed Angie and held her while we lay there in silence. Soon she was snoring softly and I was plotting on how I was going to take Alvaro all the way out the game.

Nicholas Lock

Chapter Eight

"Y'all niggas ready?" Maino asked.

"We was born ready," said G'd up, an automatic shotgun over his shoulder.

Maino and JBM were about to put the K-9's they'd gotten from Fred to use. Since the incident with Corrigan, I hadn't gotten any more folders from him, but DEA Agent Donovan was still giving them to me and to be honest I'd rather have his folders because his had bigger payouts. Corrigan had us targeting the local D-Boys but Donovan had us hitting big time D-Boys from all over. Like right now Maino, G'd up, Abdullah, Streets, Snub and Ratchet were in Detroit getting ready to hit a crew who had Detroit in the chokehold. They sold everything but their main source of income came from heroin. I wasn't there physically but I was watching via the body cams that they were wearing. Fred had given JBM top-of-the-line police gear. They were outfitted in black tactical gear with the letters DEA across the front and back.

"Let's go!" Snub yelled, walking towards one of the black Yukons.

Maino, G'd up and Streets got in the lead Yukon with the German Shepherd while Snub, Abdullah and Ratchet got in the other one.

"What are you watching?" Chell came into the living room and sat in my lap.

"My niggas about to put some work in." I pushed the laptop back so she could get a better look.

"Aahh!" She jumped off my lap away from the laptop.

"Can they see you?"

"No, girl!" I laughed. "Can't nobody see your naked ass."

Chell didn't have any clothes on so she was worried about them seeing her. She came and sat back in my lap. "And De-sire is going with me and the girls to hit the nigga Kendrick," Chell said of one of the newest additions to the team. "Shut up so I can watch this movie." I wanted to make sure shit went right.

This was the test run with the K-9 and all the tactical gear. I needed everything to go according to plan.

Boom! "D.E.A.! Get on the ground!" they yelled after kicking the door in.

Kah! Kah! Maino shot a dark-skinned dude who was reaching for a pistol.

"Clear!" G'd-up yelled, clearing a room.

"Clear!" Abdullah cleared the next room.

The training that they'd gotten from Fred made JBM look like a navy seal team. *No hustler was going to be safe from now on,* I thought as I continued to watch them move through the house, round everyone up and put them in flex cuffs.

"Y'all ain't no real police," one of the hustlers on the floor said.

"Shut up!" Abdullah kicked him in the mouth, sending his front teeth sliding across the floor.

Ratchet came in the house with the K-9 and let the leash fall.

"Find it, Missy! Find it!" he said and she took off around the house.

I watched the dog roam through the house on the body cam that was sewn into their vest. She went into the bathroom, sniffed around the bathtub, barked and sat down. Maino and everyone else knew Missy had found something. I watched as they tried to find out what had caught her nose but couldn't figure it out. Snub walked out and came back dragging one of the head dudes and sat him on the floor of the bathroom.

"What's the deal with this tub?" Maino asked him.

"I don't know, nigga! You the police, so figure it out," he laughed.

"Wrong answer," Maino said apologetically and shot him in the face.

Snub dragged him out and brought another dude in, making sure that he saw his homeboy in the hallway with a crater in his face.

"Now I'm gon' ask you the same question I asked your mans out there." Maino flashed a sarcastic grin. "What's the deal with this tub?"

He acted as if he was weighing the question then said "Turn the hot water all the way on and hit the switch for the exhaust fan."

Streets turned the hot water knob and water came rushing on but cut off when he kept turning all the way to the right. Then G'd-up hit the switch for the exhaust fan and the bathtub started to lift up.

"Oh, they did that," I said as the tub lifted all the way up to reveal a hollow space that was full of money and blocks of heroin.

I clicked the laptop close; I had seen enough. I knew what the outcome was going to be for everyone inside the house that wasn't JBM.

"I'm taking Bruno with me too," Chell said, talking about the other K-9 we had.

"And you're telling me because?" I tried to lift her off of me.

"Stop, bae!" Chell yelled and pushed back, forcing me to lean back on the couch.

She twisted around so that she was facing me. It was then that I saw the look Chell got when she was feeling freaky.

"Look, bae," she said and I followed her eyes.

My baby was dripping her love juices all over my shorts. I reached down, caught some of her juice on my fingers and brought them to my mouth.

"Let me up, girl," I said.

Chell got up and sat on the couch. I stood up and looked down at her. She was hands down the baddest bitch in the world and I had her all to myself. Her body was perfect. From her cinnamon brown skin, luscious lips, bedroom eyes to her perfectly proportioned body.

"Are you going to make love to me or are you going to just stand there?" she questioned, pinching one of her nipples.

I stripped down until the only thing I had on were socks.

"Come 'ere, daddy." Chell reached for me

I walked over to her and she guided me into her mouth.

"Fuck, Chell!" I moaned, grabbing a handful of the twenty-two-inch red weave she was wearing. Hearing me moan sent her into super head mode. Chell began massaging my balls while taking me to the back of her throat at a rapid pace. She took me out of her mouth, looked up at me and started slapping my piece on her tongue. I wasn't trying to bust yet so I pushed her away and got down on the floor between her legs.

"You gon' eat me, baby?" Chell leaned back on the couch and peeled open her puffy lips, showing me her dripping wet insides.

I put her legs over my shoulders and dove into one of my favorite meals: wet pussy.

I ran my tongue from Chell's swollen clit all the way to her butt.

"Where you going?" I grabbed her by the hips as she tried to run from my tongue.

"Unnn!" she moaned, grabbing her weave.

I began drawing eights on her clits and running my tongue around her love tunnel, causing her legs to shake and coat my face with her sweet juices.

"I love your black ass," Chell whispered drunkenly, looking at me through half closed eyes.

I put her legs down and slid my wood inside her center, making her arch up off the couch.

"I know," I said smugly, continuing to stroke her cat the way that I know drove her crazy.

I started hitting the bottom and she put her hand on my stomach, trying to control my strokes but I was on the verge of climaxing so I wasn't having it.

"You fucking the shit out of me, boy!" She tried to scoot away but I grabbed her hips, pulling her back to me.

I was a few strokes from climaxing when my son started crying upstairs. I tried to get a few more strokes in but Chell pushed me out of her and ran upstairs.

"Man, damn!" I said, getting up and sitting on the couch, holding my dick.

Chell came back down the steps carrying my son on her shoulder.

"Let me put him back to sleep and I'm gon' make it up to you." Chell looked down at my still hard member.

"Whatever." I went upstairs and got in the bed.

Twenty minutes later, Chell got in the bed and rode me to sleep.

Nicholas Lock

Chapter Nine

"No way Rai'chell knows you're over here," Sidney said, watching me come out of Laci's building.

I hadn't seen or heard from Laci in about two weeks and that wasn't like her. I wasn't used to this. Usually I was guaranteed a phone call from her. Laci was the reason I was even a free man. For me and her to only be friends/fuck buddies, she fucked with me the long way. Laci put her freedom on the line and killed a bitch for me; a police bodyguard. So, for that, I had stupid love for her.

"She don't know and she ain't gon' know," I warned her.

"Nigga, ain't nobody gon' tell on your ass," Jasmine said.

Sidney, Marquita, Tatianna and Jasmine were all standing in the breezeway of the building.

"Yea, because we don't wanna see your handsome face in the obituary section," Marquita said.

"Speak for yourself, bitch!" Jasmine sounded offended.

"What's up with your little sister, Tatianna?" I inquired.

"Don't pay her no mind, she just needs some dick," she said and all of them laughed except Jasmine.

"Y'all ready to put that work in on Friday?" I referred to them hitting the nigga Kendrick.

Kendrick was another dude Donovan had put me on. He was from New Orleans and supplied the whole state of Louisiana with gas and pills. I usually didn't go on stings anymore but I didn't trust anybody to watch Chell's back the way I would even though the girls had proven they were more than capable. But I also knew that them Louisiana niggas got super active, so I had to go.

"Don't do us! We been ready but you and Maino been bird feeding us like we not all the way with the shits." Marquita snorted in disbelief.

"That's a fact! Y'all been trying us like we're some bum ass bitches or something. To be real, JGM go harder than them soft ass JBM niggas. Them niggas couldn't hold my bloody tampon!" Sidney chimed in.

I shook my head. "It's always the pretty bitches with the nastiest mouths," I said and Jasmine's ugly ass rolled her eyes. "And I'm doing y'all, huh? Correct me if I'm wrong but didn't I make you bitches millionaires?"

"You did, big bro, but damn. How much money is enough money?" Tatianna asked sincerely.

"And we spent a majority of that already," said Jasmine.

"What! Y'all dumber than I thought," I said in a disbelieving tone.

They had all gotten four million apiece from hitting Diablo's re-up. But then again, I knew first-hand that when you got a lot of money and you weren't used to having it, that you tend to blow it. Especially when you really didn't have to work for it. Easy come, easy go. I called it the jackboy mindset.

"What the hell did y'all do with the money?" I had to know.

"We bought houses, cars and clothes. We also went to Vegas," Sidney informed me.

That kinda explained it. You could lose a hundred thousand in thirty minutes in Vegas.

"If y'all bought houses, why are y'all still over here in the jets?"

"This is just our hangout spot," Jasmine said, rolling a fat blunt of OG kush.

"And didn't you say you wanted some of this smoke?" Marquita's red ass questioned, shaking three dice.

"You ain't said shit!" I pulled a knot of money out.

We played C-Lo and smoked gas for the next few hours. In the process, I learned that Laci had gone out of town. I was going to fuss her ass out soon as we talked. I left the dice game forty thousand dollars lighter and high as hell.

***

"Bra, are you serious about this car business?" I asked Murph as we sat inside his office at his car lot.

"Hell yea. The shit is too easy plus the money is super good"

"You know what, bro? I got the club scene on lock so there's no reason why you shouldn't get the car business on lock," I told my day one nigga.

Ever since coming home and starting Jackboy Mafia, me and my nigga hadn't really been kicking it and for the most part it was by my doing. I had just been so focused on getting the clubs and dealing with all the bullshit that we hadn't been chilling. Another reason was because we weren't really robbing like that anymore. The only time me and Murph got together to rob something was when it was a big time nigga. But even still, every time JBM hit a lick, Murph got a percentage. He wasn't just my nigga, he was my motherfucking brother! My goal of controlling the nightlife in the city was complete. Now I was going to try to control the nightlife in the state but before I went all out in that department, I was going to make sure Murph took over the car business in the city.

"You're right but you know I mainly deal with the exotic cars but I could benefit from owning a couple of the regular car dealerships," he grinned.

"I know damn well you can. Stop fronting, nigga! The first dealership we need to target is Reed-Lallier Chevrolet," I said with conviction.

"Fact. I want the Audi car lot and I most definitely want Dax's on McPherson because I want to be the only one selling foreigns in the city."

"Say no more. I'ma get Ox and TNT on it asap. What about the big car lot on Skibo?"

"Damn, I forgot about that, that's Rick Hendrick. That one too. I'm not concerned with the off-brand car lots," Murph said.

"Get the paperwork drawn up and we gon' give them a chance to do it the easy way; if not, we gon' tear that bitch up."

"Bet."

"Murph, Mr. Warton is here," a light-brown skinned girl said as she poked her head inside his office.

"Oh! I'm on the way right now. Bro, he trying to buy the new Bugatti, so I gotta go." Murph rushed out of the office.

I was walking out of Murph's office when I spotted my dream car on the showroom floor.

"I'm coming back to get you," I said to the Rolls-Royce Wraith as I walked out the building.

Chapter Ten

"It's almost over, Face" Angie said, rubbing her swollen stomach. We were leaving the OB-GYN from Angie's last appointment before she dropped my daughter.

"I'm ready for you to have my little mama because you be doing too much damn running."

"Hush!" She blushed. "You know you can't be trying to go deep like that with me being eight months pregnant. You be trying to put a dent in my baby's head."

"You was running from this dick before you got pregnant. So what happened when you went to your people's house?" I referred to her going to Alvaro's house.

"Nothing, really. He got some money transferred to my bank account so I can go buy us a bigger house. And I got one picked out already. I'm just waiting on the paperwork to clear. It's a four-bedroom, four-bath two-story Georgian-style house. Overall, it's gorgeous!" Angie gushed.

"Us, huh?" I reached over and rubbed her thigh.

"Yes! You know you're gonna be there all the time and it's got a huge basement that I'm going to turn into a man cave." Angie moved my hand between her legs.

"You better stop, woman, before you make me wreck," I said, feeling the heat coming from her box.

"Just drive, baby." Angie did a half-smile, getting up on her knees and leaning over the console.

She unzipped my Gucci jeans, pulled my pole out and tried to swallow it.

"Mmhm!" I palmed the back of her head.

"Baby," she said, licking around the head. "I want you to rob Alvaro and kill him." Angie sucked my balls into her mouth. All I could do was nod, I couldn't talk. I could barely drive.

"I'm going to make sure you know," Angie took me to the back of her throat two times, "everything you need to know." She took me into her mouth again, causing me to pull over at McDonald's and lean my seat back.

"So that way you'll be able to get all the way off." Angie held me in the back of her throat as I released inside her mouth.

"Damn, Ang! I love your ass!" I looked down at her.

"You better, nigga." She licked her lips, cleaned my wood off and put it back inside my jeans.

"Why do you want me to kill him?" I knew it had to be a reason for her change of heart.

"Because me being around him brought back memories of my mother's death. And like I told you, to me he's the reason she's dead, so I want him dead!" she said adamantly.

"Look, Angie." I held her face in my hands. "I need you to realize what it is you're saying because there's no coming back from death."

"I do." She looked me in the eyes with eyes that had a hate in them that I'd never seen.

"I got you, baby, just get me the information I need and I'ma send him away from here."

I couldn't believe how lucky I was. The lick of a lifetime had just fell in my lap with a bow on it. I was going to hit Chief then follow up with Alvaro and fall back.

***

"You some real bullshit!" Ogun's little ass yelled when he saw me.

"What are you talking about?" I laughed.

"You don't fuck with us anymore." He mean-mugged me.

Ogun was only thirteen and stood 4'0 but he was one of the most ruthless TNT members they had. Ogun didn't have an off button; he only knew one mode, and that was go mode.

"You know that's a lie. Ox came back home so it was only right that he took back over TNT. Where my boo at?" I joked.

"Who?" he asked, twisting his charcoal black face up.

"Oshun," I grinned and he charged me.

I snatched his little ass up and put him in the full nelson.

"I'm gonna fuck you up!" he threatened.

"It don't look like it." I swung him around.

"Put my brother down, Face," Oshun's angelic voice said.

"Or what?" I asked and she raised one of her brows.

"That look might scare them but it don't scare me." I stared at her short, pretty self.

Oshun was seventeen now but was still barely pushing 4'0, and she had the mind of a forty-year-old. Oshun had let me know when I first met TNT that she was a dwarf. Her dark skin, high cheekbones and full lips gave her a sweet, regal look but she was anything but sweet. Oshun was a silent killer! She was a fool with knives or anything sharp for that matter. And she never ever raised her voice. Oshun could throw a knife through your eyes from thirty feet away. She was in charge of the Tiaras like Ox was in charge of the Turban gang; together they made TNT which stood for *Turbans and Tiaras*. Oshun pulled one of her knives out and started tossing it from hand to hand, looking my way.

"You might want to put him down," Ox warned, moving to the other side of the room.

"Ain't nobody worried about Oshun little—"

Thwack! The knife she had in her hand struck the wall by my head, cutting my sentence off. I dropped Ogun and rushed her before she could throw another one. I grabbed her up and tossed her over my shoulder which turned out to be a mistake.

Not only did all the Tiaras rush me but Oshun managed to turn her body around so that she was sitting on my shoulders with one of her knives to my neck.

"You got it, you got it." I laughed.

I knew Oshun wouldn't really hurt me. Even though we didn't really talk, I could tell she liked me.

She hopped down and sat on the couch. We were all at the split level across the river that I let Ox stay at. He had turned it into TNT headquarters.

"So if they don't agree to sell, we get to terrorize they shit?" Ox asked.

"You already know, so I'll be hitting y'all up soon to let you know what it is." I walked towards the door and caught Ogun mugging me. "Come on with your pouting ass."

Me and Ogun walked out the house and were getting in the Escalade I'd just bought when Oshun came walking to the truck. She didn't say anything; she just climbed in the backseat. Oshun was super protective when it came to her little brother, so I wasn't really surprised at her appearance. I pulled off with no real set destination. I was just driving.

"Do you smoke?" I looked at Ogun and he smiled and nodded. "Roll up then." I tossed him some kush and a game blunt.

I looked in the backseat and Oshun was shaking her head. I started to say something to her but I knew I probably wouldn't get a response.

Woop! Woop! An undercover in a Charger blue lighted. All my paperwork was legit so I pulled over. Officer Bernstein, one of Corrigan's flunkies, got out of the Charger and I relaxed.

"Long time no see Face," he grinned, standing at my window.

"Are these your kids?" Bernstein questioned, looking at Ogun and Oshun.

"What up? Why did you pull me?"

"Oh, yea, that. Corrigan told me to give you this," he drew his gun and was bringing it up to shoot when a knife appeared in his throat.

I burnt rubber, getting away from the murder scene. I looked in the rear-view mirror and Oshun was looking out the window as if nothing had happened, like she hadn't just murked a cop, and Ogun continued rolling the blunt as if it was no big deal. Meanwhile, my mind was going a million miles a minute. Had Corrigan acted alone or had the Elite sanctioned the hit? Either way, if they wanted smoke, I was about to give them all the smoke they wanted.

Nicholas Lock

Chapter Eleven

I was on the way to the Weeks to see what was good with Corrigan and to find out how much the Elite knew about the attempt on my life. I was passing the County jail when I saw Ms. G sexy ass getting out of her purple Charger. I made a quick U-turn, pulled into the County and blew my horn to get her attention. When she saw that it was me, she ran over to the driver's side of my car.

"You ain't shit!" She pointed a finger in my face through the rolled down window. I took her finger into my mouth and sucked on it. "Eww! You nasty."

"I know you're about to go to work—"

"I can call out," she cut me off.

"Nah, because I'm on the way to handle some business but call me tonight and we gon' chill."

"Don't be bullshitting, boy," she warned.

"Just hit me up and I got you. That's my word." I gave her my number and swerved off. I had to keep her on my team. She was definitely an asset.

I pulled into the Weeks' driveway and got out of the car. I knew they were going to keep it real just off the fact that me and their daughter had kicked it. Before I could knock on their door, Mrs. Weeks opened it, pulled me inside and slammed the door behind me.

"I already know why you're here and there was nothing me of Billy could do about it. Corrigan pressed the issue so hard that we had to vote and we lost." Courtney led me to the kitchen.

"Where's Billy?" I glanced around.

"He has trial this week. No one else is here."

I nodded. "So, if Corrigan is the problem then killing him is the solution, right?" I sat down at the round kitchen table.

"It's possible or it could make you enemy number one. The only person that can really call it off is Ryan, and he just left. He probably won't be back for a few months. He's back in Texas." Courtney handed me a bottled water from out of the fridge.

"So, what do you suggest?" I asked.

"I honestly can't answer that. This type of situation has never happened before. I know I don't have to tell you to watch your back. We're on your side, we're just not going to allow Corrigan to use the legal system to get you out of the way, either. But please don't underestimate him, he's extremely cunning and sneaky."

"Not as cunning as me," I reminded her as I stood up to leave. Then, something came to mind. "Who all voted on my side?"

"Me, Billy, Tasha, Donovan, Liu and Consuela."

I nodded and walked out. I was surprised to learn that Tasha had voted in my favor. Corrigan was in for a rude awakening, and with Donovan being on my side I would still be able to get licks for JBM. I was about to show Corrigan he wasn't the only one who had shooters.

"Okay, here's the deal: Chief's main spot is in Red Springs but his two stay houses are in Lumberton and Maxton. But check this out—he lives in Fayetteville. It's out there in Baywood." Wolf gave us the scoop.

"So, how do you want to play it?" Murph questioned.

"I'm with whatever," Wolf shot back.

I hadn't voiced my opinion yet. I was more occupied with rolling a blunt.

"Why don't we hit his house first. That way, he won't be alerted when his spots get hit?" Ogun wisely suggested.

I had brought Ogun with me to show him another hustle other than terrorizing people. I had really taken a liking to

Ogun and Oshun. It took a lot of convincing but they had finally relented and allowed me to take Ogun with me without Oshun tagging along. But she let me know that if anything happened to him, she was going to cut me up into a million tiny pieces. Chell played a huge part in it also; she was taking Oshun with her so that they could hang out with the girls.

"That sounds like a plan." I sparked the blunt.

"Let's get to it then," Wolf was anxious to hit Chief because he knew if we pulled it off successfully, he would be straight financially for years to come.

"Look, we gon' hit his house because I'm sure he has old money there. We can also hit the stash spots, but why not let some of JBM hit his main spot? Because it's a lot of work for us to hit four houses in one night," Murph offered.

"That'll work," I said, calling Abdullah.

"What up, bro?" he answered.

"I'm about to text you an address. Get G'd up and Streets and hit, take Bruno."

"On it." He hung up.

We strapped up in the D.E.A. flak jackets and AR 15s. Then, we drove the twenty minute-drive out to Chief's neighborhood and cruised by his house.

"How we doing this?" asked Wolf.

"Police-style." I parked the Durango and we all piled out of the large SUV just like real federal agents. "Throw the flash grenade!" I barked.

Boom!

The explosion was loud and bright. We kicked in the front door of the house and rushed in.

"D.E.A.! D.E.A.!" we yelled authoritatively, as we ran through the house.

Ogun encountered a panicked Chief in the hallway. He dropped the nigga with a round from his AR. We rounded up the wife and children and sat them in the living room, not far from where Chief lay.

"Chief, this can go one of two ways. It's up to you. Where is everything at?" Murph took control of the sting.

"Fuck y'all! Do your job."

"And what exactly do you think our job is, sir?" Ogun joined in the fun.

We all were rocking ski masks, disguising our true identities.

"Police-ass mutherfuckers," he spat. "Hurry up so I can post bond. Pussies!" Chief spat.

"Make bond, huh? I didn't know you could make bond from the grave. I snatched my mask off and saw Chief's whole expression change.

"Surprise!" taunted Wolf, pulling off his mask to Chief's horror.

"I told my sister you was a snake ass nigga!" Chief snorted.

"Fuck all that! Where's the money and work?" Murph said.

"I don't know."

I went outside to the truck and opened the backseat. "Come on, Missy." I called to the K-9. The dog hopped out, tail wagging. The female beast followed me back into the house and the second Chief saw the dog he started sweating bullets.

"Find it, girl," I commanded.

The dog took off sniffing around the house. I sat down in front of Chief's wife. She was a skinny white girl with big breasts. She hadn't uttered a word the entire time; she was just hugging the children close to her body.

"Tell me where it's at and I'll let y'all live," I said gently, but she just stared at me without speaking a word. "You taught her well," I said to Chief.

At that moment, Missy began barking, letting us know that she had found something. I rushed to the den where the dog was at. I found her sniffing by the entertainment center. Behind the flat screen I found a single brick of dope. *This can't be all that's here!* Fuming, I carried the brick into the living room and sat it on the coffee table in front of Chief.

"This all you got here?" Murph asked after seeing the paltry stash.

"That's all." Chief smirked.

Ogun grabbed a crystal elephant from the table and slung it against the wall. "Stop playing games!"

I looked at the hole that was now in the wall and a thought came to mind. Following my suspicion, I walked over to the wall and looked inside the hole. What I saw brought a smile to my face. I looked back at Chief. "You sly devil."

I pulled the cheap dry wall apart all the way down to the floorboard.

"Damn!" Wolf let out a long whistle after seeing dozens and dozens of vacuum sealed money. Chief had money stacked inside the wall from the floor to eye level.

Ogun, Wolf and Murph started tearing down the other walls in the living room. I grabbed one of the packs of money and tore it open. There was nothing but stacks of hundred dollar bills. "This that old money," I smiled. "How much is in each pack?" I asked Chief, not expecting a response.

He surprised me by replying, "A hundred thousand."

I let out a long whistle. Like I said, Chief had been supplying the entire Robeson County for many years. And Robeson was the largest county in North Carolina. I estimated there was at least a hundred packages piled up on the floor and my team was still pulling more out.

My phone rang. It was Abdullah.

"What's up, bro?" I answered.

"Face, we hit big! Eighty pounds of gas, thirty bricks of coke, thirty bricks of heroin and a hundred rivals in cash," he said.

"That's y'all's. Enjoy yourselves. But I want some of that gas," I said.

Abdullah laughed and hung up.

Wolf and 'em had all of the money out of the walls and stacked in bundles of ten. That shit looked like a maze. I quickly calculated that it was twenty million; each of us would get five million dollars.

"I appreciate it, Chief," said Wolf, then he raised his gun and blasted Chief twice in the head. The kids screamed but Chief's wife only squirmed.

I looked at Wolf and raised my brows. He nodded and then sent the mother and children wherever Chief had gone. It was a bloody scene, but I knew we couldn't have spared their lives.

I called Maino and gave him the address to the stash house in Maxton. I told him to take Ratchet, Snub and Rico with him. Then I called Chell and told her to take the girls and hit the stash spot on Lumberton. All of my team was going to eat if I had something to say about it.

As Ogun and 'em loaded the loot into the truck I set the house on fire. As we drove away, all I could think about was how was Pocahontas going to take her brother's death.

Chapter Twelve

Fall had snuck up on me. The grass had turned brown and it was starting to get chilly. This was good for me but it was horrible for D-boys. Fall and winter was the season I called hoody season, aka jackboy season. This was the time of the year when I really got on my bullshit with regard to robbing. At the moment, I had on a black Champion hoody, some black joggings and a pair of black Air 1's. I was on war time.

"Where you at?" I asked Ross.

"I'm pulling up right now," he said and I saw him pulling into IHOP's parking lot.

I shook my head as he got out of the Blue Urus.

With a huge smile, Ross got in the new Charger I was driving.

"I thought I told you to keep a low profile, at least until I can take care of Corrigan."

"Fuck the pig! I got plenty of bail money," Ross boasted, causing me to shake my head.

Ross thought Corrigan was just a Narc but he wasn't aware of the type of power or the kind of connections he had.

"Furthermore, I got Sha Loc and a car full of shooters dying to prove their loyalty and what better way than to kill the head Narc in the city?" He looked at me.

"I don't see no car full of shooters." I looked around.

"Are you supposed to?" Ross grinned.

Then I saw them. I had seen them when they had pulled in but they had pulled in twenty minutes ago. The minivan they were driving had took them off of my radar then there was a woman behind the wheel.

"Yo, my nigga." I turned to look at Ross. "Why the fuck was they here twenty minutes before you?" What are you trying to say?"

"It ain't even like that. We all left at the same time but I had to go back so I told them to go on ahead. You're bugging!" he said in a disbelieving tone.

"Oh, a'ight. Look, bro, Corrigan isn't to be taken lightly, he has a lot of connections. Just lay low until I can get him dealt with because I can almost guarantee you this. If he somehow manages to get them handcuffs on you, you might not see freedom ever again," I said to him seriously.

Sha Loc's Pepsi blue Challenger pulled up beside me and he got out and walked to my side. I rolled my window down and Sha Loc said, "Cuz, I hope you talk some sense into that nigga. He thinks he can take on the head narc in the city. A dirty narc at that"

"I'm talking to him but–" I stopped when I saw the line of Chargers pull in.

I crunk the car up and took off!

"What the hell you doing?" Ross yelled.

"Them Charger boys coming!" I looked back and seen two of the Chargers pulling out of the IHOP.

The Charger boys were a part of the V-CAT squad. V-CAT stands for Violent Criminal Apprehension Team. They didn't play any games. I knew when they pulled in that they were either there for me or Ross or both. And I didn't plan on staying to find out. I got off Skibo Road and onto Bragg Boulevard. I wasn't worried about them catching me. I was trying to get out of sight so I would be able to outrun their radios. Their Chargers were V-8's but mine was a V-12! I had just bought her two weeks ago and had her upgraded just for situations like this.

"There go another one!" Ross pointed as another Charger came out of nowhere.

"We straight!"

I got off the Boulevard and onto Martin Luther King freeway. The V-12 hummed to life as I pressed the gas pedal to the floor. They didn't stand a chance. I left the three Chargers behind. There wasn't a doubt in my mind whose doing it was that the V-CAT squad had chased me.

"You still think Corrigan is to be played with?" I looked over at my day one as I drove us to safety.

Corrigan thought he was untouchable. He must've lost his mind because he knew I got super hero active! I knew he knew that I was coming but he didn't know when, where or how. Corrigan had switched his car up. He drove a black Camaro now; he couldn't know that I knew already or he would've switched again. It didn't matter anyway because I had set Tyrone on him. Tyrone said he was trying to get down with the team and since he was in the army and had access to all types of exclusive shit, I told him to smoke Corrigan's ass. I let Tyrone know the place he was guaranteed to go was the police station beside town hall; all he had to do was wait. I was at the Airborne Museum watching when Corrigan's Camaro pulled out of the police station. Tyrone had been parked along the road sitting in a gray Mustang waiting for him. So when Corrigan's Camaro pulled out, Tyrone got out of the Mustang with a rocket launcher. Corrigan saw Tyrone and tried to swerve but Tyrone let a grenade fly from the rocket launcher. The grenade struck under the back wheel, flipping the Camaro three times. It landed on its roof ablaze. Before Tyrone had a chance to get back inside his car, he was swarmed by the Charger boys as if they had been waiting. When they hopped out, Corrigan got out of a red Charger. They had been waiting! He had set a trap for me. Corrigan had almost outsmarted me. He knew the station was where I was going to try and hit him; he just hadn't expected me to send someone else. It was nothing I could do but watch as they slammed Tyrone to the ground, put cuffs on him and put him in the back of one of the Chargers. And if Corrigan hadn't been in the Camaro, then who was?

Chapter Thirteen

"So you're not coming with us?" Chell woke me up.

"I thought you were a big girl. You want me to come watch your back, huh?" I teased because she already knew that I was coming on the lick with them.

Plus I wanted to see Desire in action; this was going to be her first time hitting a lick with the girls. Initially, Desire was going to be on Jackboy Mafia but Chell had snatched her and put her on Jackgirl Mafia. They were one and the same, only the Jackgirl Mafia consisted of only chicks.

"Anyway, I just know you're not gon' let me go hit no sting without you there." She crawled under the covers with me.

"You're absolutely right. You're so right that you need to let everyone know that this is your last one. You're about to hang your ski mask up. You need to focus on having my babies." I pulled her to me and kissed her.

"And you're going to hang your ski mask up too, right?" Chell rubbed her hand over my face.

I looked her in the eyes and said, "I got one more sting. After I hit it, I'm gonna hang my mask up but I'm still gonna be orchestrating shit."

"And you're going to cut off all your hoes and put a big rock on this finger."

"Of course."

"No, nigga, fo' real for real. I know yo' still got some hoes out there just like I know you and Angie fucking. No, don't get up," Chell told me because I had sat all the way up.

"Nymel, I'm far from dumb. I been knew but I also knew that your future was with me. Besides, I came to the conclusion that you're going to fuck bitches. I also know that I'm the wife."

Nicholas Lock

I didn't really know what to say, so I didn't say anything. She hadn't said anything about whose baby Angie was about to have. I assumed she knew.

"Is everybody ready?" I climbed out of the hotel bed.

"All the girls are in the lobby already," Chell informed me, letting the conversation we had just been having go. I quickly got dressed, and me and Chell went downstairs. The girls had seen us and didn't acknowledge us; they just walked outside to the U-Haul. I walked out and got behind the wheel of the black Escalade that the K-9 Missy was in while Marquita drove the U-Haul. Tatianna and Desire rode with me and Rai'chell. I was peeping Desire's demeanor; she was the wild card. Desire's young ass had to earn her stripes. I was looking at her in the rear-view mirror. She was easily one of the prettiest dykes I had ever seen.

"Something wrong with your eyes?" Our eyes met in the mirror.

I started laughing. "You talking to me like that? You gotta be high."

"Nigga, you looking at me." Desire rolled her neck.

"That's because I was trying to see if I saw any signs of pussy or nervousness."

"Pussy? I got one and I eat it but I'm not one. And in this business you don't have time for feelings of nervousness. Nervousness leads to being indecisive which can lead to the grave or jail and I don't know about you but I'm not willing to see either," Desire gave it up raw.

Her answer put me at ease. I just needed to see her in action. We rode to the outskirts of New Orleans to bring Kendrick down. Kendrick was a tall brown-skinned older dude. The folder said he was forty-seven, lived alone and didn't have any children. He was making it easy for us because beside his house was another two-story house that belonged to

70

him. It was the spot he held all his work, which was sorta genius because who'd expect a half a million-dollar house to be full of drugs.

"Park down the street, let them go ahead." Chell gave me instructions.

I was letting Chell call all the shots on this one. I was mainly a spectator in case something went wrong or didn't look right.

"So what's about to happen?" I was curious to know what Chell's plan was.

"They're going to act like their U-Haul broke down and go knock on his door. I told Sidney to get him to let her in but if not to take him down in the door."

As she was giving me the rundown, I saw Sidney get out of the U-Haul.

Goddamn!" I said when I saw what Sidney had changed into.

Pop! Chell popped me in the head. "Don't get fucked up."

Sidney had my undivided attention. She had put on a pair of orange boy shorts and a white crop top. But the shorts only covered half her ass and, every step she took, her ass would jiggle uncontrollably. Sidney would cause a traffic jam on I-95 right now. I didn't believe in doing dirt in my backyard but Sidney was making me contemplate trying to fuck her. She knocked on Kendrick's door and the instant he saw her, he let her in which was a mistake on his behalf. Two minutes later, Sidney opened the front door and waved us over. Marquita backed the U-Haul up to the stash house and they all got out. When we walked in the house, Sidney had Kendrick on his couch with his hands tied behind his back.

"Y'all must don't know who it is you're robbing," Kendrick said in a heavy New Orleans accent.

"All you need to do is tell me where everything is at so I don't have to do any unnecessary work. And that includes where everything is at next door!" Chell said and his eyes narrowed.

"Bitch, suck my dick!" he spat.

I walked out the room to look through the house. They were more than capable of handling the situation. I didn't even see the point of talking to the people we hit anymore. The K-9's would take us to the drugs but it was Chell's sting, so it was what it was. I made my way upstairs and found my way to Kendrick's bedroom. He was a total slob; he had clothes everywhere and old food scattered all around the room. I left his room and walked back down to the living room only to see that the girls had stripped Kendrick naked. Chell squatted down in front of him and put a Taser between his legs.

"Rrrr!" He groaned as the electricity shot through his body.

"Damn, girl!" Tatianna watched Chell work.

"You had enough. Are you ready to talk?" Chell circled him.

I looked over at Desire to see how she was reacting to everything and she was standing there with a bored look on her face. Then my eyes drifted over to Sidney in her booty shorts. *I want some of her loving*, I thought to myself, glancing at her exposed ass.

"Bae, go get Missy," Chell said.

I went and grabbed the K-9 and let her loose in the house.

"Tell the devil I send my regards." Chell raised her pistol.

"Nah, hold up. Why not let the new girl do it?" I voiced my opinion.

Desire looked at me, like, *Nigga, you ain't said shit*. She walked over to Kendrick and put his thoughts all over the wall. I nodded in approval. There wasn't any work in his house but the spot next door yielded six hundred pounds of gas and too many pills to count. We loaded the U-Haul up and I followed behind them until we got back to Fayetteville. I dropped Chell, Tatianna and Desire off with the other girls and left. I didn't have a stake in their sting. I was doing good for myself, plus I knew what was Chell's was mine.

Chapter Fourteen

"Face, I need you to help me find out who did it." Pocahontas paced back and forth in my office.

Pocahontas was in my office at *Pleasure's,* trying to get me to help her find out who had killed her brother.

"Pocahontas, what are you going to do if you find out who it was? Huh? These are grown man games." I tried to talk some sense into her.

"I'm definitely not going to put the police on them. You see this pretty face and fat ass and think I don't get active. I'm from the swamps, nigga! I can get real savage!" she snapped.

Pocahontas was so worked up that she was turning red.

"Sit your ass down. You getting yourself worked up for no reason. And what gives you the impression that I can find out?" I folded my hands behind my head and leaned back in my chair.

"Really?" She squinted. "The streets talk, Face. It ain't too many people in the city that don't know who you are and what you do." Pocahontas told me something I didn't know.

"And what exactly is it that I do?"

Pocahontas paused like she was weighing my questions.

"You rob and you're a killer." Pocahontas stared me in the eyes as if she was trying to read my thoughts.

"You got me all wrong, Poca. I'm just a business owner."

"A business owner that has a team of jackboys under his control and a crew of young reckless kids that only want to kill something." She let me in on the fact that she knew a lot about me.

I wasn't too concerned about what she knew about me. I was more concerned about who had told her. And my guess would be Wolf's pillow-talking ass.

"Look, whoever did it, if they're about their business, you'll never know. Because to speak on it to anybody would for one be dumb and, second, it incriminates them. And to my understanding, your brother was a somebody, so for him to be able to get at your brother, he's no dummy. I'm gon' reach out though and see what I can find out but I'm not promising you a thing"

"Thank you!" She ran around my desk, hopped in my lap and hugged me.

"Get off of me, girl."

She got off me as my phone started to blow up. I looked and saw it was Angie.

"What up, boo?"

"My water broke! I'm on the way to the hospital!"

"I'm on the way."

I rushed out of my office and ran into Danielle.

"Face, you're going to make me come hunt you down." She grabbed me by the shirt.

"Not right now but I'll be back later."

I left and rushed to the hospital. When I got there, Angie had just received an epidural.

"You good?" I asked her and she nodded.

Angie was in labor for twelve hours. She had my daughter at 4 o'clock in the morning. We named her Angelique. She had Angie's hair and nose but my complexion and my lips. I stayed with Angie and my baby girl until the sun came up. They were both asleep when I left. Seeing my daughter made me want to see her grow up and live life. I had to get rid of Corrigan so I could ensure that I was going to be alive to see it.

"Baby, your face is all over the news! They're saying that you put a hit on a narcotic detective!" Chell yelled into the phone.

"I'm gonna call you back." I hung up and called Lauren.

"What's up, America's most wanted?" she joked, letting me know she had seen the news.

"Let me use one of your cars. The jakes are going to be looking for mine."

"Come on."

I drove to Kings Grant, the neighborhood Lauren stayed in. When I pulled up to her house, she was standing in the door in her housecoat.

"Which one do you want?" She let me in.

"The Challenger. I might need to get low."

Lauren's black Challenger was custom made. The car topped out at 250.

"You owe me for this, nigga." She handed me the keys and opened her housecoat, showing me the white teddy she had on underneath.

Any other time, I would've fucked her all through the house, but my freedom was in jeopardy, so my mind was elsewhere.

"I know what you need but my mind on these charges, Lauren. Let me figure this shit out and I'ma come nail you to the bed."

"I understand. Oh, and Chino told me to tell you he needs you to take care of one of his enemies for him."

"Huh?" Tell him I'm not one of his soldiers! That's dead! He better send some of them cartel members." I was done doing shit for everybody else! It was time for me to start focusing on me. The whole while I had been robbing I had been making sure my team was good. Now it was time to make me the number one priority.

"Damn, don't shoot the messenger."

"Lauren, the messenger always get shot," I said and left.

I had to get things in order. It was Saturday, so I knew Tasha was at her house. Tasha had a condo in Parkview Manor which was the crème of the crop when it came to condos in Fayetteville. Every condo was in the four-hundred-dollar range and better. She didn't even know I knew where she stayed. If Mrs. Weeks hadn't told me that Tasha had voted in my favor, I wouldn't even be approaching her, especially since we had been bumping heads since we met.

I parked and got out. I pulled my Black Lives Matter hoody over my head and walked in. I took the steps to the top floor and knocked on Tasha's door.

"Gimme a second!" she yelled through the door. "Oh my freaking God!" she shrieked when she opened the door.

"Move!" I pushed past her.

"You cannot be here," she said, closing the door.

"Well, I am." I started going through her house to make sure we were alone.

'What do you think you're doing? You can't just barge in my house and go through it like you pay bills here!" Tasha protested.

"Look, yo, I'm not here to hear your mouth. I need you to find out what kind of evidence they have on me or is this Corrigan's doing?" I took a seat on her California king sized bed.

"Make yourself at home," she said sarcastically "And no, this isn't Corrigan's doing. We're not allowing him to manipulate the system but I might've shoulda."

"Shut up! You know you fuck with me on the low. Now what do you know, *Ms. I'm-the-best-lawyer-on-the-east coast*?" I threw the words she told me when we first met back at her.

While she thought of what to tell me, I noticed for the first time that she was wearing a short silk robe. Tasha being 6'0, the robe was about six inches above her knees. This was my first time seeing her outside of business suits and now I saw why she always had them on. Her redbone ass was strapped. Tasha was so thick it was ridiculous. I felt my dick rocking up, so I focused my attention elsewhere.

"Your homeboy told on you," she dropped a bombshell on me. "He told them you paid him to do it."

Nah, Tyrone wasn't living like that. He was one of my niggas for real.

"The worse thing you can do is tell me a lie about my nigga." I got up off the bed and walked to where she was leaning up against her dresser. "Because I won't have an issue pushing that sew-in sideways." I got in her face.

"Ain't nobody lying to you, Face, and back the fuck out of my damn face!" She lightly pushed me in the chest. "And what the hell do I benefit from lying? What are you doing, boy?"

I lifted Tasha up and sat her on the edge of the dresser.

"I'm getting comfortable." I stood between her legs.

"Get comfortable somewhere else." She pushed me again in the chest but like the first time it was a light push. I had lost all train of thought. The vanilla scent coming off of her body had me in a trance. The silk robe Tasha had on had rode up so that I could see between her legs. I looked up at her and she was just staring at me. I unbuckled my pants and pulled my dick out. I rubbed the head up and down her wet center.

"You sure?" I asked, placing my pole at her entrance.

Tasha grabbed my ass and pulled me into her.

"Face," she moaned.

"Damn, you so wet!" I gritted my teeth, continuing to plunge inside Tasha's love box.

"You gon' make me cum all over this young dick!" Tasha closed her eyes and yelled, lifting her hips every time I went inside her.

Hearing that sent me into overdrive. I started trying to knock the back out of her pussy when I glanced down at her dresser and saw a government I.D.

"The fuck!" I stopped mid stroke.

"Why you stop?" She opened her eyes.

I pulled all the way out, pulled my pants up, grabbed the I.D. and drew my gun.

"Let me explain, Face."

"Please do because my knowledge tells me you're a lawyer but this clearly says: *Tasha Garland, C.I.A.*"

"Okay, listen," she paused. "No one is supposed to know this but I kinda like you and like I told you before, you have a mind unlike the average eighteen-year-old. Plus I'll deny telling you anything. And unlike the Elite, the C.I.A will make you disappear with ease," she stated seriously.

"So you are a C.I.A agent?" I questioned.

"Yes. I've been undercover for the last three years. I've been tasked with taking down the Elite."

Chapter Fifteen

I was stuck in a tight spot. Tasha made me promise not to blow the whistle on her and, in turn, she was going to make sure that I would be able to kill Corrigan. Fuck it!

"We can't fuck this up. This will probably be our last legitimate shot at killing him," I told Ogun and Oshun.

Since Corrigan's flunky had tried to kill me, they felt like they were my bodyguards, especially Ogun. Everywhere I went, they wanted to go. They had for the most part moved in with me and Chell. After the Chief lick, I took Chell house shopping and, as expected, she picked the biggest house she could find. Chell must have been eyeing the mansion for a while because she directed me right to it. It was a six bedroom, six-and-a-half bathroom, four-car garage mansion. It had a gym, an Olympic style ground pool, and a movie theater.

Once I found out that Ogun and Oshun were living with their aunt who was hardly ever there, I didn't mind them staying with us. Then when I found out that they were sending a majority of the money that they were making to their parents in Africa, I really didn't care. Ogun and Oshun were from Ghana. Their parents sent them to the States for a better life and education. They had six other children to care for and, with Ogun and Oshun being the most independent, they didn't second guess sending them. It was there that Oshun learned to throw knives or anything sharp for that matter. With her being the oldest, it would sometimes fall on her to get the family something to eat, so her knife throwing came in handy.

"I want this to go as smoothly as possible," I told them.

We were on the way to Corrigan's house. Tasha had given me his home address.

"It's easy. When y'all ring the doorbell, all they're going to see is two kids standing on their porch. They won't see a potential threat. They should just open the door."

"I'm not a kid. You're only a year and a half older than me!" Oshun said. "So if I'ma kid, so are you."

Since moving in, Oshun had started talking more. I was starting to miss the old Oshun.

"Your short ass know what I mean," I said and she pushed me in the back of the head. "Look, I want that entire house dead! Even the goldfish, nothing lives."

"This is my kind of party," Ogun's bloodthirsty ass said, checking his baby '9.

I parked four houses down from Corrigan's two-story brick house and watched as Ogun and Oshun walked up to the house. A black lady answered the door and immediately let them in. I just shook my head because she'd let the devil's kids into her home. Five minutes later, Ogun and Oshun came strolling back to the car.

"What happened? Was Corrigan there?"

"I caught him in the shower and that's where he died at," Oshun said proudly.

"I killed the woman and knocked the fish tank over," Ogun added.

I texted Tasha and Mrs. Weeks and informed them that there was an opening in the group. They would understand. Now I had to figure out how to deal with Tyrone and I had just the remedy.

***

"I shouldn't even have answered your call," Ms. G. said after she opened her door.

"Yea, right! You know damn well you want some of this good wood." I slapped her on the ass as I walked by. All she had on was a *Forever 21* t-shirt that barely covered her ass, so she already knew what time it was.

"Come on," she led me to her room in the back of the house.

I sat down on the edge of her bed and she straddled my lap.

"So what took your ass so long to call me?" Ms. G. pushed me in the chest so that I was lying flat on my back.

She took off the t-shirt and stared at me. Her thirty-seven-year-old body was banging! Her D cups sat up high and perky and she had a fat, plump booty that was just right for her slim frame.

"You like what you see?" Ms. G unbuckled my belt and unzipped my jeans.

I didn't reply; instead, I lifted my hips so she could take off my jeans. She got the message because she pulled my semi-hard dick out and put it in her mouth. I grabbed a handful of her lace front and started forcing her to go all the way down.

"Fuck that! Watch out."

I got up and bent Ms. G over the bed. I grabbed a Trojan out of my jeans, put it on and slid into her.

"Mmm!" she moaned.

I started pounding her out. I wasn't trying to make love.

"Nah, that ain't happening," I told her as she started trying to run.

I grabbed her by the back of the neck so she couldn't run, and started back dragging her.

"Face! Unnn!" Ms. G yelled.

"This is what you been asking for, so take it," I gritted my teeth.

Her pussy was talking to me, making me go harder. I was trying to hold off but her pussy was top notch. All of a sudden her pussy got real wet.

"I'm cumming!" she yelled.

I pushed all the way in and sprayed my seed inside the condom.

"You make me sick." She lay down on her stomach.

"Aww, man!" I groaned when I pulled out.

"What?" Ms. G turned over and saw the broken rubber. "Boy, you good. I'm clean, nigga."

"I pretty much know that. I just don't need you getting pregnant." I pulled the broken rubber off and tossed it in the trash.

"Anyways . . ." she crawled up under the covers.

I got in the bed with her and she put her head on my stomach.

"Yo, I need you to handle some shit for me," I said, rubbing my hand up and down her back.

"What?" she asked lazily.

"I need you to put something in somebody's food for me. I'm gon' give you a quarter million and a vacation to wherever you wanna go."

"Damn, boy, you paying me like you want me to kill somebody."

I didn't say anything and she popped her head up.

"You want me to kill somebody for you?" she asked incredulously.

"It won't be traced back to you, I promise," I said with confidence.

"Who is it? Wait, I know who it is. That dude that tried to kill that detective!" she said out loud. "Oh, nigga, you think you slick!" She punched me.

"What are you talking about?"

"I'm not stupid, boy. After that dude got locked up, they put your face all over the news saying that you put a hit on that detective. And now you want me to kill him so he can't tell on you." Ms. G put the pieces to the puzzle together.

I was impressed.

"That's really the only reason you even called me." She punched me again.

"Nah, I really wanted some of this pu—" she cut me off.

"Save the lies for your hoes. I want half a million and you got to buy me the new Mercedes AMG," she made her demands known.

"It's yours, gangsta," I quickly agreed.

"Just let me know what I gotta do and how to do it. Oh and I almost forgot. You gotta bring me this dick whenever I want it," she said and went under the covers to suck me back to life.

It was a small price to pay because you couldn't put a price on your freedom.

Nicholas Lock

Chapter Sixteen

"Rai'chell know we be fucking," I told Angie while I watched her feed my daughter.

"So what? She'll be okay. She was going to find out eventually. Besides, I'm allowing her to have you because I could make it to where you're only mine but I get that dick on command, so I'm straight," Angie said nonchalantly.

"Don't say it like that. But anyways, what's up with me hitting Alvaro?" I needed to know if she was still with me on robbing him.

"Oh yea, here, burp her." Angie handed me Angelique.

I put my daughter on my shoulder and patted her back to burp her while Angie went in the back. Every time I held my daughter, it did something to me. She was so little and fragile looking. I would die before I allowed something to happen to her.

"Okay, so look, this is the house Alvaro stays in." Angie showed me her phone.

"You went all out, didn't you?"

Angie had taken pictures of Alvaro's mini mansion from every angle imaginable. This let me know how serious she was about the lick. Alvaro's mansion was two-stories and from the pictures it had seven bedrooms.

Outside the property there was a twelve-foot white brick wall that enclosed the entire property.

"Where the hell is this at?" I couldn't place the house or the surrounding area.

"It's a suburb on the Hoke County line. There's only seven houses and they're spaced out so far that you don't have to worry about anyone seeing what's going on." Angie continued giving me details.

"What exactly does he have there, Angie? I don't need to be on no dummy mission." I cradled Angelique, putting her to sleep.

"As of now he doesn't have anything but he's about to get a major shipment in the next month. He's planning on making Fayetteville his main distribution center."

I thought to myself for Alvaro to do that would mean that he not only would have a lot of work but money as well. I could care less about the work now because Ross had a legit plug on the work, so I didn't have to worry about helping him get on anymore. I wanted the money!

"I got you, woman, just let me know when the shipment gets here and he's a done deal," I reassured her. Me and Angie were sitting in her living room when someone knocked on the door.

"You expecting company?" I asked her.

"No," she shook her head.

I got up and walked to the front door. I opened it and there stood Domonick.

"Where's Angie?" He brushed past me.

Oh, he had his people fucked up!

"Motherfucker, are you dumb? Or do you just want to die early?" I fumed and he just stared at me with a smirk on his face.

I pulled the Smith and Wesson .357 and his smirk turned into a frown.

"Shit real now, huh? This ain't Colombia. You don't run or control shit over here, pussy!"

"Nymel, stop!" Angie yelled, making the mistake of stepping between us.

See, Angie knew how I really gave it up from stories but Chell knew from being there first-hand. That also meant Chell knew the rules of engagement. So she would have never got in my way when I had my fire trained on somebody. And the reason being is exactly what happened. While Angie was between us, Domonick produced a gun of his own.

"Oh my God, Domonick!" Angie put her hand on the gun Domonick had in his hand.

She got him to lower his gun. I had to give her credit for that but she knew better than to try me like that. *Pow!* I slapped him with the .357, dazing him then put it under his chin.

"Please Nymel! Your daughter is in the other room," Angie begged.

Angie saying that kinda brought me back to reality because I was about to blow the top of Domonick's head off. My only dilemma was that I didn't believe in pulling out guns and not using them. Not only did I not believe in it, it was against the law. *Boom!* I shot him in the leg, causing him to crumple to the floor.

"You fucking pussy!" He gritted his teeth while holding his leg.

"The next one will be to the face!" I warned him and walked out.

***

"What up, Lauren?" I answered my phone.

"Where are you at? I need to holler at you"

"Riding up Bragg Boulevard."

"Meet me at the McDonalds. I'll be there in about five."

"Who was that?" Ogun questioned me when I ended the call.

"If your nosey ass must know, it was my homegirl Lauren."

Me, Oshun and Ogun were cruising around the city chilling. I was informing them about how in a day or two we were going to run down some car lots so Murph could take over the car business. When I pulled into the McDonalds, Lauren was sitting on the hood of her BMW.

"Look, Chino is in town and he wants to have a sit-down with you." She got right down to the matter at hand.

"For what?"

"He didn't say. He just said he wanted to meet with you in person."

"Where at?"

"K and W. He rented the whole cafeteria so it's only going to be y'all," Lauren said.

"A'ight."

I followed Lauren to the K and W by the Cape Fear Valley Hospital, and we got out. I wasn't worried about anything crazy because Ogun and Oshun lived by the mentality of shoot first, ask questions later. There were Mexicans scattered throughout the parking lot and inside the building. Chino had a table that was located in the far right corner with a smug looking Karla sitting beside him. I was really starting to dislike Karla. She was sitting on her high horse but didn't know that I could easily knock her off of it.

"What's good?" I asked, not bothering to sit down.

"I need you to handle that business for me it's the—"

"Chino, it's clear that you have the wrong idea about me so peep this, I'm not a mercenary, a hitman or your do boy. I don't owe you anything, bro. Get one of your people to do it."

"I told you he wasn't shit." Karla rolled her eyes.

"Bitch, you might want to stay in your place before I put you there!" My blood started to boil.

Oshun moved by my side while Ogun moved to where his back was a few feet off the wall.

"Karla, stay the fuck out of their business!" Lauren said, seeing that the place was about to get bloody.

Me and Chino locked eyes. I could tell he was used to being the only shot caller in the room.

"Face, *no* isn't an answer that you can give. You do owe me."

I started laughing. "Chino, this meeting is over. Let it go, Chino, because to press the issue is going to cause a lot of bloodshed."

"He just threatened to kill you! Kill him!" Karla screamed then fell out of her chair holding her throat.

Nobody but me, Oshun and Ogun knew what had happened. Karla stood up on wobbly legs. When she moved her hand, she had a deep gash on the side of her neck.

"That was your first and only warning, the next one goes through your throat. Let the men handle their business," Oshun said in her low, angelic voice.

I was done with the whole situation so I started walking out with Ogun and Oshun behind me.

"I'll be seeing you around, Face," Chino said to my back, I kept walking. There was no reason for me to comment. I was formulating a plan in my head that would keep Chino busy for a while. When I got in my car, Lauren sent me a text that said: *I'm on your side.*

Nicholas Lock

Chapter Seventeen

"You got a lot of explaining to do, Laci," I said into the phone. She had finally called me.

"Oh, you missed me?" I could hear the smile in her voice.

"I wouldn't dare blow your head up like that. Now where the fuck your ass at?"

"Wherever you want my ass to be." She dropped her voice. I looked over at Ogun and Oshun playing with Missy, wondering how I was going to duck them. They already were in the mindset that they were my protectors but since the run in with Chino, I couldn't go to the bathroom without one following me. Chell thought the shit was cute.

"I'll be at your spot in about thirty minutes." I ended the call.

I got up and walked into my bedroom. I changed out of the jogging shirt. I walked out the door in my bedroom out to the backyard. I walked around the house to the front yard where I had the Porsche parked and Oshun was sitting on the hood.

"Going somewhere?" she asked.

"Go ahead, Oshun. Y'all ain't got to be with me 24/7."

"Says who?" She got her short ass in the car.

Fuck it! She wanted to come, that was on her but I was going to make sure she rethought coming with me the next time.

I pulled up to Laci's apartment building and got out with Oshun beside me. I half expected to see the girls out shooting C-lo but they were nowhere to be seen. Before I could knock, Laci opened the door and blew my mind. She was no longer the big girl I was accustomed to seeing and her body was out of this universe.

"You like?" She spun around smiling.

I walked in her apartment with Oshun behind me and Laci's smile faded when she saw her.

"Who is this?"

"My little bodyguard." I looked at Oshun who was staring Laci up and down. "Come on." I grabbed Laci's hand and went down the hall to her bedroom.

I sat on the edge of her bed and grabbed her by the hips.

"I went to Dr. Miami and got all this done." Laci rubbed her hands along her body.

Laci was wearing one of my wife beaters that I had left at her house and she was making it look good. It looked like she had gotten poured in the beater.

Laci's 5'5 caramel colored frame was now rocking a pair of perfectly shaped melon sized breasts, a nonexistent stomach and an ass that would make a monk take a second look.

"So you went to Miami and ain't tell nobody?" I couldn't stop staring at Laci's new addition.

"Mmhm." She pulled the wife beater over her head. "But I'm back now and I'm here to claim what's mine." She straddled my lap.

"What's yours?"

"You." Laci whispered, putting her tongue in my ear causing my little man to stand up.

"Laci, you know I got a girl," I reminded her as she undid my jeans.

"She temporary." Laci lifted up and put me inside her warm walls. "Fuck me, Face!" Laci yelled.

I didn't have a remark at the time for her comment about Rai'chell being temporary because her insides were massaging my dick in a way that had me speechless.

***

"Food cart in the block!" Tyrone yelled.

Tyrone was being held in special management which was nothing but the hole. Once word got out that he wasn't living right, everybody wanted a piece of him. TNT members were even getting locked up and sent to the hole to try and get at him. For his safety the mayor had him put in protective custody.

"Shut your police ass up!" Nuka yelled out his door.

"Tell your mama to shut up, fuck nigga!" Tyrone shot back.

"Nuka! Fuck that nigga, he a mock! He a dead man walking, Lacurtis said.

"Ms. Gipson sexy ass in the block passing out trays. Ms. Gipson, I need an extra tray today," Tyrone said.

"Don't give master splinter shit!" Nuka told her.

She could only shake her head and continue to feed the block.

"Ms. Gipson, when I get out, I'm coming to get your pretty black ass. We gon' make some pretty babies." Tyrone spat his game.

"Boy, you not gon' be thinking about me when you get out. You all talk." She smiled. "Here, boy." Ms. G gave him an extra tray from the cart.

"Yo! I can't believe you fucking with that rat ass nigga. You do know that he's the one telling on Face?" Lacurtis inquired.

Lacurtis didn't personally know me but he had heard of me. He hated rats. He was facing a life sentence because of a nigga telling on him. Ms. G. left out the block to go feed another block while they ate.

"I hope you choke on that shit, nigga!" Nuka was keeping it hot on Tyrone.

Tyrone had just finished his second tray when Ms. G. walked back into the block. Seeing Tyrone had smashed both trays, she looked at Lacurtis and said:

"Just so you know, Face was at my house last night fucking the shit out of this pussy, ass and mouth."

Tyrone heard her statement and tried to walk to his door but fell flat on his face, foaming at the mouth. Ms. G. grabbed the two trays off his food port and closed it. She had put the cyanide pill in Tyrone's chili. It was just enough to kill him but little enough so that it wouldn't be detected in his system. They didn't find Tyrone's body in the floor until three hours later but by then he was long gone. When Ms. G pulled into her driveway that night, Ogun and Oshun were waiting for her. They killed her fast per my request. I knew if shit hit the fan, she would fold; so to prevent that, I sent them to eliminate the possibility. With Tyrone out of the way, my name would be clear—no witness, no conviction.

Chapter Eighteen

"You got a rabbit's foot up your ass, boy," Tasha said into the phone. With Tyrone dead I was able to get the warrants on you pulled back."

"A'ight, good." I ended the call.

I was leery of her now that she'd told me she was in C.I.A.

"What the fuck ever, Dantarius!" Diqueena barged into my office with Ross on her heels.

"Y'all can leave all that Jerry Springer shit at the door!" I warned.

"Shut up, boy," Diqueena walked around the desk and gave me a hug. "Hey, Murph. Sup, Wolf. Go ahead, there he go." She turned on her heels to face Ross.

"I don't need no help, girl. Anyway, Face, I think you might need to holler at your peoples," Ross told me.

"My people, who? And about what?" I was lost.

"Some of my spots have been getting hit and the only people in the city with those kinds of balls is the team you got."

"Huh?" I looked at him like he was crazy. "Ross, every sting my people hit, I know about it and most of the time I'm the one who orchestrates the shit," I said.

"Don't no other jackboy in the city got it in them. Niggas know how I give it up!" he said assuredly.

"My nigga, you tripping! You're making it seem like you're untouchable. If a nigga get hungry enough, he'll try and do anything to eat. Nigga, lions try elephants when their ribs start touching." I was starting to feel like he was trying my thug.

"Bra, just holler at your peoples," he said again.

Oh, he had me fucked up! I was about to get in his shit when my office door busted open and Pocahontas barged in.

"You pussy ass, bitch made ass nigga!" Pocahontas poked Wolf in his forehead. "I should have known your young ass ain't shit!" she screamed.

"Yo! Take the relationship problems home," I said.

"These ain't relationship problems! This bitch ass nigga is the one who robbed and killed my brother! And your bitch ass was probably with him!" She glared at me.

"Let that be your last time calling me a bitch and I don't know what the fuck you're talking about. Take a deep breath and calm down." I tried talking to her. I needed to find out what the hell she knew, how much she knew and how she found out. Her last statement let me know she didn't really know if I was directly involved or not.

"Damn, y'all deep in here." Lauren walked in.

"Don't tell me to calm down when the motherfucker who killed my brother is sitting right here!"

"What gives you that impression?" I questioned her.

"Bro, she bugging," Wolf finally spoke up.

"This!" She held up a big gold ring with an Indian chief in the middle with green diamonds all around it. "I was doing laundry and it fell out of one of his coat pockets."

My jaw almost dropped but I kept my composure. I couldn't believe Wolf had slipped like that. That was a rookie mistake.

"Why wasn't I invited to the party? Hey, sis!" Chell said to Diqueena as she walked in my office followed by Ogun and Oshun.

"Wolf doesn't have the gumption to have done this alone so your bitch made ass had to have put him up to it if you weren't with him!" She directed her gaze back towards me.

"Who the fuck she calling a bitch? Not you." Chell looked at me.

"Chill, yo." I needed to diffuse it before things got out of hand.

"Fuck you too, bitch!" Pocahontas made the mistake of saying.

Before I could get around my desk, Diqueena and Chell had fired on Pocahontas. She fell and they started to stomp her out. One of the girls that Pocahontas had hired peeked her head in the office and saw them stomping her out and decided to try and help. I grabbed Chell up, and the girl drew back to hit Diqueena, but Lauren hit her with a five piece that buckled her knees. Then Oshun ended her stripping career because when she hit the floor Oshun straddled her and began carving her face up until it looked like hamburger meat.

"Man, grab them!" I yelled.

Ross grabbed Diqueena and Wolf tried to grab Lauren and she started firing on him. It was pure chaos in my office.

"Put me down, Face!" Chell shrieked and I let her go but I pulled my hammer.

Boom! I let off a shot in the floor.

"Everybody, get the fuck out now!" I was stupid mad. I hated being around stupid shit. Pocahontas helped the stripper chick out of my office and most likely to the hospital, if she didn't bleed to death on the way. Everybody started filing out of my office, even Chell. She knew when I was dead serious. I sat down at my desk and looked up and Lauren was still standing by my door.

"Bye!" I said.

"Boy boo." She took a seat on the couch. "You need to hear what I have to say anyway. Chino wants to make Fayetteville his stronghold in the south. He's already starting to set up shop. He's been shipping in cartel members from Mexico for anybody who gets in his way. Your name hasn't been brought back up but I know for a fact that he wants you dead."

"Fuck Chino. Let him try his hand and I'll send him home in a box. And as for him setting up shop, that doesn't mean shit to me because I don't hustle. I rob. You said you was on my side so when he try his hand I expect you to put me in a position to kill him."

"What's understood never has to be explained," Lauren said and walked out of my office.

Chapter Nineteen

"You already know that though and it can't be a small fry because Ross's operation has a nice set-up," Maino informed me.

"I figured as much. How you living though?" I asked. Me and Maino were posted up at the park on Deep Creek Road smoking and chilling.

"Shit pretty my way. It's pretty for the whole Jackboy Mafia right now. These last few months have put us so far up that we've been mingling with the Angels. You're about to see!" he bragged.

On cue, seven exotic cars pulled into the park. It looked like a mini car show. Snub pulled up in a blue AMG GT-R, Rico pulled up in a gray Ferrari 812 super-fast, Streets had a blood red Viper GTS, Abdullah drove up in n the new Maserati MC20, G'd-up had a black Rolls-Royce Cullinan, and Ratchet was in a burnt orange Bentley coupé.

"Murph gave the squad a deal on these shits as soon as they came in; they didn't get a chance to hit the showroom floor," Maino said.

I dapped everybody up as they exited their cars.

"Hands on my knees shaking ass on my thot shit!" Megan Thee Stallion rapped.

We all turned towards the sound and saw six pink Porsche 911 GT3 RS's

"Y'all thought y'all were going to leave us out!" Chell hopped out of one of the pink Porsches followed by Sidney, Desire, Jasmine, Marquita, and Tatianna.

"The jackgirls is here!" Tatianna yelled, getting out.

"Okay!" Sidney cosigned, putting her hands on the hood of her car, twerking.

All the girls got out and started twerking to the music. Chell knew better than to shake her ass; she came and stood by my side.

"Sidney fat to death!" Abdullah said, watching her twerk.

"Not like Tatianna chocolate ass," Rico said.

"Put y'all tongues back in," Chell told them.

"So everybody living good I see. All y'all got foreign and shit. Everybody got jewels and a smile. This the kind of shit I like to see." I smiled.

"We all need to hit the club together and have fun. I'm in the mood to shake my ass enough," said Sidney.

"You don't think you done shook your ass enough?" I said and she gave me the finger. "Before we get to the pleasure, let's get to this business. I need to find out who it is that's been hitting Ross's traps."

"We'll check into it and I'm with Sidney. Let's hit the club. We ain't never all went out together," Marquita commented.

"I like that idea but how about next week? And I can make it an all-black party," I said, trying to see how I was going to get TNT in, then it occurred to me that I owned the club.

So I could do what the fuck I wanted!

It took more than a week to get everything set up because at first, I was having the all-black party at *Club Aqua* but after all the requests for VIP passes, I moved it to *Pleasure's Paradise*. Why not make some money in the process and my girls would ensure that niggas spent plenty money! Plus I was turning it into my birthday bash as well. A nigga was turning nineteen. I just wished my twin was here to celebrate with me. I had just gave Angie fifty bands just because. She told me to leave the streets alone because I had a legit thing going and she didn't want to have to come see me in prison or a casket. I told her I was good and left.

Not only was the whole Jackboy Mafia going to be in attendance but TNT as well. God forbid a nigga or bitch acted up. Tonight I ain't deadening shit!

"Happy birthday, daddy!" Chell walked in the bedroom in a red lingerie set with the nipples and crotch area open.

"Come sit on my lap." I looked at the way she was posing by the door with her left foot over her right.

Chell bit her lip and slowly walked over to me.

"You better be glad I love you, nigga." She closed her eyes while I ran my finger between her legs.

I pulled my dick out of my balling shorts and Chell hopped up.

"Nope, I got a surprise for you first." She grabbed my hand and led me out of the bedroom.

Chell made me follow her through the house to one of the guest rooms. When I walked in, Sidney was laying sideways in the bed with no clothes on, brown skin glistening. I watched as Chell walked over to the bed and palmed Sidney's ass.

"You scared of this pussy or something?" Sidney asked, lifting her leg and dipping her finger inside her sex.

I stripped down and put my pole at Sidney's entrance. I looked over at Chell to see her reaction and she reached down and guided me into Sidney's love tunnel.

"Shit!" Sidney's box had me gripped as if she had her hand around my dick.

I started to long-stroke Sidney while Rai'chell straddled her face. Watching Sidney eat my bitch sent me over the edge. I sent a load of my kids into Sidney.

"I know the fuck you didn't!" Sidney looked at me.

"Be like that sometimes," I smirked.

"What the fuck ever!"

"Shut the fuck up," I said, "and take this dick."
I hadn't gone soft, so I began to stroke her again.
I fucked Chell and Sidney for the next three hours.
When it was all said and done, we all fell asleep in the bed
sexually satisfied.

***

"Where you at?" Murph asked.
"I'm walking out the house right now, bro." I ended the
call.
I was running late because I had to convince Oshun to
come. She wasn't a fan of large crowds. Ogun, however, was
so eager to go that he'd been ready and dressed hours ago. I
checked myself out in the mirror one more time and nodded.
I was wearing a black Chanel V-neck, black Chanel belt, some
black Chanel shorts and a pair of black Chanel sneakers. I had
taken the all-black theme to heart. I had a two-inch-thick
bracelet made and it was flooded in black VVS's. Then I had
lost the first Carolina Panther chain I had, so I had a new one
made and it too was flooded in black diamonds with blue diamonds for eyes. It was black, everything I had on! The diamonds in my grill were even black.
"Y'all come on." I walked in the garage.
"What we riding in?" Ogun questioned.
"Oh, you don't know?" I smiled and he shook his head.
Oshun walked over to the all-black Wraith. I had finally
got the motherfucker! I had just pulled her off the showroom
floor two days ago. I hadn't really drove her yet but tonight
was the night. We got in and I was about to pull out when
Ogun yelled:
"Wait, wait!"

He hopped out the Wraith and dashed back into the house. Me and Oshun looked at each other and shook our heads when Ogun came back out the house carrying an AR15 with the monkey nuts connected to it.

"It's lit!" Ogun yelled when we pulled into the parking lot and saw how long the line was.

Everybody outside was watching the Wraith, wanting to see who was about to get out. I pulled up to the front of the club and parked. Soon as I got out of the Wraith, Maino walked out of the club and I started laughing. He had on a black t-shirt with the words *You make it, we take it* across the front, and on the back it said *Jackboy Mafia*.

"We got a shirt for you too, nigga! The whole team is wearing them. TNT got shirts too," Maino said.

We walked in the club and everybody mobbed us. I saw the TNT shirts and they had *TNT* across the back but the front had a picture of Osama bin Laden with the words *Terrorizer* under it. Somebody threw me a JBM shirt and I put it on while Ogun and Oshun put on TNT shirts. I looked around and saw we were deep as hell! Almost everywhere you looked, you'd see either a JBM or TNT shirt.

"Come on. We got a VIP booth." Murph led me away to where Chell and all the girls were.

The girls had the same shirts we had except the back of theirs said: *Jackgirl Mafia*. I looked at Sidney and she smirked before turning her head away.

"Happy birthday, baby!" Chell kissed me on the lips.

"You getting old, nigga," Diqueena joked.

"Get the fuck out of here, girl. Where Ross at?" I asked her because I needed some more intel on his spots getting hit.

"He on the way," Diqueena informed me.

"Can I get everyone's attention?" Murph had went and grabbed the mic from the DJ. "I'd like to propose a toast to my brother, the birthday boy, Face. Everybody, put your bottles, glasses, or something in the air for this toast." I walked to the edge of the VIP booth and looked over at Murph by the DJ booth and shook my head. He was always doing some crazy shit.

"There go the birthday boy right there," he pointed and everyone looked my way.

I nodded, smiling.

"Yo," I answered my ringing phone.

"Face, you need to get out of there!" a frantic Lauren said.

"Huh? What are you talking about?" I put my finger in my ear trying to block out the noise.

"Get out of there! Chino sent a suicide death squad to kill you!"

Lauren's words rang in my ear as the shots started. I looked towards the entrance and saw a flood of Mexicans rushing through the door. I watched as one of them shot Ratchet in the back of the door.

"Get down!" I yelled to Chell and pulled my Glock out.

Boc! Boc! Boc! I sent death towards the oncoming ese's.

It was hard to get a clean shot off because the club goers were going crazy trying to get away from the bullets.

"Come on!" Chell yelled, pulling my arm.

"Fuck that!" I shot one of the Mexicans that was trying to come up the steps.

My niggas were putting up a fight but it was a losing battle. There were too many of them plus we were outgunned. I pointed my hammer at an ese and pulled the trigger. *Click!* I looked and my gun was empty. He raised his AK my way and a knife hit him in the forehead, killing him. I looked to my left and saw Oshun.

"We don't have any wins," she mouthed to me.

If Oshun was saying this, then there was something to it.

I grabbed Chell and took off running. Being that I was the target, all the ese's focused on me. I pushed Chell off to the side and ran to the back. I ran out the back door and into Oakdale.

Kah! Kah! I heard the choppa bullets whizzing past my head. I looked back and it looked like a mini army was chasing me! I ran into Oakdale apartments. I knew if I made it to the cut I was good.

"Aah!" I yelled as a bullet creased my side.

I kept running, holding onto my side. I knew if I fell, I was done deal. *Skrr!* I looked back over my shoulder and saw my Wraith coming with Ogun shooting the AK-15 and Oshun throwing her knives. Then I saw a green Escalade bend the corner. Maino, Abdullah and G'd-up were in the SUV gunning the Mexicans down and the girls were in their Porsches letting their guns talk. With them out in the open the death squad had nowhere to run, so my team easily mowed them down. Chell pulled the Wraith up and I hopped in.

"Oh my God, you're hit!" she yelled.

"I'm good, it only grazed me," I said, lifting my shirt to look. "Did everybody make it?" I asked and the car got dead quiet.

"They killed the whole JBM except Maino, Abdullah and G'd-up. All the girls made it though. A good portion of TNT got killed too," Chell muttered.

"What about Ox?" I wondered.

"He got hit in the leg but he's good," Ogun said. I sat back in the seat thinking Chino had taken half my team out in one swoop but he'd fucked up by not killing me. Now I was about to show him the error of his ways.

Nicholas Lock

Chapter Twenty

After the incident at *Pleasure's Paradise*, I was trying to lay low and get things in order. Me and Maino paid for all the funeral so the families didn't have to come out of their pocket for anything. All the while, I was plotting my get back and I think I had it figured out.

"Cuz, I need to holler at you asap," Sha Loc said

"Shit, where you at?" I asked.

"Kickback Jacks."

"I'll be there in about twenty." I ended the call

"Who was that?" Oshun questioned.

"Sha Loc."

Oshun and Ogun were already overprotective but now they were overbearing. I couldn't front though; with them, around I knew I was just about untouchable. I would get retarded but us three together was too much!

I pulled up to Kickback Jacks and we all got out. My head was on the swivel. I was confident Sha Loc wasn't on no bullshit but I still had to be cautious. The rich nigga hoody I had on hid my features; I was on my incognito shit. I wasn't even driving my cars. I was driving rental cars, and even those I switched up every couple of days. We walked in and I immediately spotted Sha Loc; he had a table in the far left corner. He had on blue from head to toe. He got up when I walked up to the table and we shook up.

"What's the deal?" I asked, sitting down with Ogun right beside me and Oshun beside Sha Loc.

"I don't know any other way to tell you this," he paused, looking me in the eyes. "Ross set you up at the club on your birthday night."

I got up and walked outside. I couldn't breathe! My chest felt like an elephant was sitting on it.

"Ain't no way!" I yelled to no one as I walked around the parking lot.

"It is a way," I heard Sha Loc say from behind me.

I turned to see him, Ogun and Oshun standing there.

"The motherfucker Chino came to Ross the other day telling him how he was about to set up shop and that he could either get on his team or die. Chino told him he had to set you up to prove his loyalty," Sha Loc told me and I started throwing up.

I literally couldn't stomach the fact that Ross had turned on me. Ross was one of the last niggas I expected to flip the script. Besides Murph, he was the only other nigga I considered a brother, him and Sha Loc. I had really put him on. I had gone to war with Rude Boy over him, which in turn caused my twin to get shot up and lose his football career, then his life. I had shed blood, sweat and tears for him and he repays me by setting me up to get killed.

"What's up, cuz? What you gon' do?" Sha Loc asked.

I looked at him. I knew what he was asking but I couldn't bring myself to tell him to kill Ross. I knew all I had to do was say the word and it would get done.

"I don't know yet. I gotta clear my head. I'll hit you up in a few." I opened the door to the F-150 and got in followed by Ogun and Oshun.

"I understand that Ross was your day one but you *have* to kill him or either get him killed," Oshun said softly.

"What makes you say that?" I was curious to know.

"To not kill him would show the others inside your circle that they can get over on you without any repercussions," she stated wisely.

"Let me do it," Ogun volunteered.

"I would but I need it done slowly so he can see the error of his ways and you don't know what that means. You'll just want to shoot him in the head and be done with it."

"So who are you going to get to do it?" he questioned and I shrugged.

I cut on Boosie's *Betrayed* and I cruised through the city, lost in thought. Ogun and Oshun sensed I wasn't in the mood to talk because they stopped talking and let me brew in silence.

"Where you at, bro?" I asked Murph on the phone.

"At the house, why? What's good?"

"Grab Maino and meet me at J.W. Coon." I ended the call.

I pulled up to the elementary school and got out with Ogun and Oshun close behind me. I walked over to the playground and sat on the slide. This was one of the spots me, Murph, my twin, and Ross use to come to chill and smoke. Murph pulled up with Maino following behind him. They walked over to where I was and posted up.

"What the hell do you got us out here for? I was in the middle of something," Maino said.

"I gotta plan that I'm going to need y'alls help with. Y'all know Chino has set up shop in the city but so has the Medellin Cartel. I'm trying to pit them against each other. Look, we're going to snatch up some of Chino's men and kill them. Then we're going to raid one of the Medellin's spots and in the process leave the bodies of Chino's men so that they'll assume it was them. That way they'll go to war with each other. While they're warring with each other we should be able to knock them off." I laid down the plan.

"Sounds like a plan to me," Maino agreed. "Now if you don't mind, I got a pretty, red bitch waiting on a G."

"Man, get your horny dog ass outta here," I said. "Murph, Ross switched sides on us. He playing for team Chino now," I told him after Maino left.

"Yea, right," he said in a disbelieving tone.

"Same thing I thought but this came from Sha loc. Chino approached Ross on some get-with-the-winning-team type shit or die and he went for it." I shrugged.

"What you trying to do?" He searched my face.

"He gon' get his. I want to handle the big fish first and save him for last."

"Say less."

Chapter Twenty-One

"I don't know. All he said was he wanted all of us here so I got everyone here," Mr. Weeks said to us. Ryan Bush wanted all of the Elite at the Weeks' house. I was off in the corner watching everyone. I was still wary but obviously Corrigan wasn't that well liked. They all acted as if nothing had happened and me killing him was no big deal but I was still on point. Then with Ryan calling a meeting so suddenly, I was on guard. I had two guns and a bullet-proof vest on. If they came for me, I was going to take at least half of them with me. Ogun and Oshun were mad that I wouldn't bring them with me.

I looked around the table and for the first time I realized that I really didn't belong. Plus I didn't really fuck with them. Well, I fucked with the Weeks but that was by default. I couldn't lie, I kinda fucked with Tasha, I just had to figure out her motives.

"I wish he would come on. I got somewhere to be!" Mayor Curtis complained.

"And I got a press conference to attend," the Chief of Police added.

I once again found myself wondering what the fuck I was doing in the Elite. Yea, they had the legal system on lock but that wasn't helping me with my current situation. I rubbed my hand down my face. I was only nineteen but I was starting to feel like I had the weight of the world on my shoulders.

"You look stressed." Tasha walked over to where I was.

"I'm good, what about you?" I looked her up and down.

Tasha's tall red ass was looking good in a white short set. I looked at her thick thighs and thought of the day when I was between them.

"I'm good, thank you for asking," she used her white tipped finger to lift my head up so that I was looking her in the face. "But I've never seen you so quiet. What's on your mind?"

"Heavy is the head that wears the crown, Face." Ryan stepped out of the shadows. "I bet when you decided to be a boss, you didn't know about all the bullshit that came with it. From the haters to the envy to your closest friends turning on you," he said knowingly. I only nodded and watched Tasha's ass as she walked back to the table.

"I know y'all are probably wondering why I called everyone here on such short notice. Well, it seems we have a minor problem. Someone in this room is playing both sides of the fence." He paused to allow his words to sink in.

It took everything in me not to look at Tasha.

"Someone in here has been speaking on the Elite, telling things that shouldn't be said." He walked the table.

I laughed to myself as I watched Ryan walk around the table in his white tuxedo with the black bow tie. You could tell he was a boss. Not because of the way he dressed; it was his aura. When he walked in a room, you knew. A lot of people be under the illusion that because a nigga got to the bag, that made them a boss but nah, that wasn't the case. It was plenty of niggas that had money but were nobodies and didn't have the respect of their peers. You knew a real boss even if you weren't one just like a fake nigga knew a real nigga when he saw one.

"Who do you think it is, Face?" he asked.

"I have no clue," I said and me and Tasha locked eyes.

Tasha was trying to keep her composure but I could see her sweating.

"I saw something in you the first time we met. You remember I voted you in the group immediately. The rest of the group will bite their tongue when it comes to me but not you," he said, continuing to walk around the table. "Then

you're decisive. Once you make a decision, that's what it is."
Ryan stopped behind the Chief of Police.

"Face, kill him. Mark here has been talking to the wrong
people about the Elite."

"Now wait one minu—"

Boom! Boom! I put two hollow points in his chest, sending
him to the afterlife.

"How many times do I have to tell you guys that I know
everything! Just like I know you're at odds with Chino." He
looked my way.

"Nothing I can't handle," I said assuredly. He shrugged.
"That concludes our business for today. I'll be back in a couple weeks. In the meantime, we need to replace the members
we recently lost. When I come back, I expect y'all to have
some people lined up." He walked out. There was nothing left
to talk about, so I left too. I had shit to handle.

Nicholas Lock

Chapter Twenty-Two

"You need to get down here to *Pleasure's* right now!" Sidney yelled into the phone.

"I'll be right back," I told Angie.

"No! Wherever you're going, I am too." She went to grab my daughter's diaper bag.

I looked at Oshun and Ogun and they were smirking. They never left my side nowadays, so they had met Angie and she loved them. She didn't know that they were ruthless killers. We all got in the Navigator rental with Angie in the back with my daughter. When I pulled into the parking lot, there were several police cars around the club.

"What's going on?" I got out and walked up to where Sidney was.

Since the incident with Pocahontas, I had hired Sidney to manage the clubs. She had a bachelor's degree in business administration.

"Pocahontas bitch ass! She changed the locks and everything!" Sidney said.

"Calm down, I got it."

I walked up to the front of the club as Pocahontas was coming out.

"I want him off my property too," Pocahontas said, causing me to look around because I knew she wasn't talking about me.

"Sir, we're going to have to ask you to leave," one of the cops said.

I laughed. "I own this club."

"No, he doesn't, look! Pocahontas hurriedly pulled some papers out of the clutch she had and gave them to the officer.

"Sir, it says she's the sole owner of this club and several others."

"Say what? Let me see that." I snatched the papers out of his hands and started reading them.

I looked up from the papers and looked Pocahontas in the eyes. We locked eyes for a brief second then she looked away. I don't know how she did it but she had gotten all the clubs put in her name. I winked at her and walked away.

"What's up?" Sidney questioned.

"Call and tell Chell I said *smoke that bitch.*"

"What happened, babe?" Angie asked.

"I let my guard down once again and let somebody in too close and they snaked me." I pulled off. "It's all good though. Anyway, I'm gon' be handling your people real soon."

"I can't wait. I'll be able to sleep so much better."

"In due time, in due time."

There was just too much disloyal shit going on, so I needed to relieve some stress. Me, Murph, and Maino were about to put a piece of my plan in motion.

"Y'all niggas ready?" I hit the ZaZa-filled backwood.

"Is that a real question?" Maino questioned, pulling his hoody over his head.

"I'm probably more ready than you." Murph took a swig of Hennessy.

"Let's go then." I hopped out of the stolen Charger. I was on my bullshit! There was a bar on Yadkin Road that a bunch of Chino's men frequented and this was where we were going to snatch a few of them up from. I walked right into the bar. The minute I stepped inside, everyone got quiet. All eyes were on me. I looked around the bar and all I saw were hardened faces. That alone was going to make my decision that much easier. I turned around and walked back outside. I did a quick little two step, trying to put some distance between me and the bar. As I knew they would, three of Chino's men walked out of the bar.

"Aye, homes," one of them called after me.

I looked back and they started speed-walking, trying to catch up to me.

"What up?" I stopped.

"You fucked up, my friend" he said and they started circling me.

Pow! I lunged and punched him full in the mouth and he ate it! I was used to my hits dropping niggas. He smiled a bloody smile and rushed me. I caught him with a quick two piece that stumbled him. I turned as the other two rushed me swinging haymakers. I swung, hit the bigger of the two in the side of the head and thought I broke my hand. They pinned me up against the wall and started pounding on me. All I could do was try to protect my face.

"The next one who swings will die where he stands," I heard Murph say and cock his pistol. I regained myself and pulled my own gun out.

"Put your hands behind your back!" I was mad as fuck! "Bra, put the flex cuffs on them" I told Murph.

"Ha, ha, ha!" Maino cracked up laughing. I looked and saw Maino leaning up against a truck smoking a Newport.

"Glad you're entertained!" I glared at him while I rubbed my side.

My shit was sore as hell!

"*Entertained* ain't the word. You had it all under control. Plus I knew you was strapped. And you was looking like you needed to get that off," he continued laughing.

"Maybe I should let them get a hold of you," I warned.

"You could but I ain't doing no fighting."

I shook my head and helped Murph put them in the trunk.

"Where to now, Ali?" Maino joked.

"Remington." I laid back on the backseat.

The Colombians had set up one of their stash spots in up-scale Remington. We were going to hit the stash spot and leave Chino's men. That way it, would put the Colombians and Mexicans against each other. And with them at war, it wouldn't be so hard for me to take Chino out.

Alvaro had gotten a two-story house in the back of Remington thinking it would be a good spot to hide a stash spot. He couldn't have been any wronger.

"How the hell are we going to make this happen without getting shot?" Murph inquired.

"Just chill," I said, watching the house.

A Papa John's delivery car pulled up to the stash house and out got Lauren in full Papa John gear. I had recruited her to help me. I knew we weren't going to be able to just walk up to the door without having to duck bullets. This way we could get in with minimum casualties.

"Come on," I said.

We all got out just as Lauren rang the doorbell.

"No one here ordered pizza," I heard whoever had answered the door say.

Zzzz! Lauren tased him, dropping him to his knees. We ran from the side of the house as Lauren took off to the car. Murph was the first one through the door, with me coming in last. I closed the door and tied up the man who answered the door.

"Who was at the door?" someone in the house asked. Maino and Murph went to go deal with whoever else was in the house. I was walking back out the door when the shots started but just as fast as they started, they stopped. I popped the trunk and grabbed one of the Mexicans. I wasn't worried about Maino or Murph; they were more than capable of handling the few men in the house. I dropped the ese on the living room floor as Murph came down the steps holding his side.

"What the fuck wrong with you?"

"Pussy got off a lucky shot and grazed me."

"You tripping." I walked over to him and lifted his shirt. I shook my head; he had a deep gash on his side.

"Go ahead and sit in the car. Me and Maino got it from here."

Me and Maino took the other two ese's upstairs and killed them, leaving them for the Colombians to find.

"What is that?" I asked Maino about the duffel bag he had.

"You didn't think I was really gon' leave that money, did you?" He grinned.

"Oh, nigga, you about to bust that down," I said on the way back to the car.

"We gon' drop this retarded ass nigga off so he can get his shit together and we gon' go pay some strippers bills," Maino said, reminding me that I didn't own a strip club no more.

Chapter Twenty-Three

"Face, I need you to come see me, daddy," Laci said into the phone.

"I'm kinda in the middle of something, Laci." I was on my way to scope out Alvaro's house again with Ogun and Oshun.

"Please, Face, I bet you won't be disappointed."

"I'm on the way, Laci?"

"Wait, I'm not home, I'm on the west side."

"The west side? What do you have going on, Laci? Where at on the west side?"

"I really don't know, it's a neighborhood off Raeford Road. After you pass the Walmart, make a left at the next light. Follow that road all the way around and you'll see me," she said and ended the call.

My antennas were up but my better judgment told me Laci wasn't on no disloyal shit. I followed her directions until I got to the neighborhood. I didn't even know it existed. From the looks of it, it was a well-to-do neighborhood. All the homes were upscale and most of the cars were foreign; I hadn't seen a Toyota yet! I came upon a nice two-story house with a white exterior and Laci standing in the front yard.

"Damn, she sexy!" Ogun said, eyeing Laci's stocked frame

"Watch out, lil' nigga." I laughed.

I parked and we all got out.

"Come on,' Laci led us into the house and into the living room.

"Oh, shit!" I grinned.

Pocahontas was tied up to a chair in the middle of the kitchen floor.

"Nigga, don't nobody put on for you the way I do." Laci jabbed her finger in my face. "When I heard what she had done, I made it my business to find her. So here she is. I'll be expecting a visit soon so we can discuss *our* future," she said and walked out the door.

Our future? I took a deep breath. I hoped she didn't start acting crazy.

"Well, well, well. Did you honestly think that that little stunt you pulled was going to stand up? Look at you now. All you had to do was continue running the clubs and everything would've been good. Take that rag out of her mouth." I told Oshun.

"Y'all killed my brother! You should be glad I ain't kill your motherfucking ass! Wolf told me everything! He told me how you made him do it and how you set it all up."

"First off, that ain't true but it don't matter now. This is what you're going to do. You're going to sign all my clubs back over to me and go about your life." I hopped up on the island counter.

"Why, Face! Why? That was all I had left!" She dropped her head, sobbing.

"Since Wolf told you everything else, why didn't he tell you he was the one who killed your brother? Where is Wolf anyway?"

"Right here."

Boom! Boom! Boom! Wolf came in the house dumping! I was forced to fall backwards off the counter and onto the ground.

"So this is how you repay a nigga for putting you on?" I peeked around the bottom of the island and Wolf sent two rounds my way.

"It's nothing personal, just business," Wolf said.

"I beg to differ. I think you let this bitch put that pussy on you and your stupid ass. What do a nigga got to do to get some loyalty out of you bitch ass niggas nowadays?" I came up shooting at the same time as Wolf and the slugs from my .357 Glock knocked him off his feet.

Oshun ran over and kicked his gun out of reach. Instead of walking over to Wolf, I went back to where Pocahontas was tied up.

"Look at you," I said.

Pocahontas was bleeding all over the floor, she had obviously taken a bullet during me and Wolf's exchange.

"Go ahead and sign the clubs back over to me so I can get you to the hospital," I lied, lifting her head up.

"All the paperwork is in my office down the hall in the top drawer," she croaked.

I went and got the paperwork but when I walked back into the kitchen, Pocahontas was dead.

"Fuck!" I screamed.

I walked over to where Wolf was laid out on his back with Oshun and Ogun standing over him.

"So stupid! I had faith you were going to be something but now all you're going to be is a memory." I put two more slugs in Wolf and walked out of the house. I was going to sign Pocahontas' name myself. Who was going to say if it was forged or not?

My next move was going to send a shock wave through the criminal underworld.

Nicholas Lock

Chapter Twenty-Four

"You lucky all you got was a graze, nigga." I got on Murph's ass.

"Ain't nobody trying to hear that shit. I'm trying to watch all this ass." He grabbed a stripper and pulled her onto his lap.

I shook my head. We were at my club, *Bottoms Up,* chilling. Well, Murph was chilling, I was watching Lucy. I had gotten a folder on her a long time ago. She was a scammer and was supposed to be the best in the city. I wasn't going to rob her though; I was going to recruit her to the team. The way I looked at it, scamming was the new way to rob. Plus, scamming didn't require you to put a gun on anybody, thus eliminating the risk of you having to kill somebody or somebody killing you. Another plus was the time you got behind scamming wasn't half as much as you could get for robbing or busting your gun.

"Don't you have enough women problems? And she looks like she is a definite problem." Murph followed my eyes.

"You slipping. You don't remember her?" She that scammer bitch that we had a folder on a minute ago." I tried to jog his memory.

"Oh, yeeaa!" he said, rubbing on the stripper's butt.

"And she cutting up," he added.

Lucy was definitely acting up! She was in VIP throwing money like I did when I was on my bullshit. I knew she had to be spending big boy paper because Majestic was in her section dancing, and Majestic wouldn't dance for you if you didn't have serious money. I watched Lucy throw money for a few more minutes and I got up.

"I'll be back," I told Murph and he paid me no attention. He was focused on the lap dance he was getting.

I made my way to Lucy's section and before I could get all the way up the steps, a nigga stopped me.

"Who you here for?" He stood in my way.

"Lucy. But if you don't get out of my way, they gon' be reading about you tomorrow."

"Nigga, you only got two seconds to go the fuck back down them steps before I—"

He didn't get to finish his sentence because I punched him in the mouth, causing him to fall back on one of the couches.

"What the fuck!" Lucy walked over to where we were.

"Face," she said, letting me know that she knew who I was.

"You know this bitch ass nigga?" Dude asked, getting up off the couch like he was ready to fight.

"You should too since he got all the dope boys in the city on eggshells plus this is his club." Lucy looked me in the eyes.

"You seem to think you know a lot about me, yet I don't know anything about you!" I shot back.

"Fuck who he is; he about to get his issue!" Dude said, walking in my direction.

"Sheem, let it go, I got this." Lucy signaled for me to follow her. "Y'all, let me talk to him real quick," she said and everyone in VIP walked out.

I was secretly impressed but I knew when you were the breadwinner, people would treat you like the Pope.

"Whatever it is, I'm with it," Lucy offered after we sat down.

"You don't even know what it is I was going to say. How do you know I'm not here to ask you to sell pussy for me?"

"For one, that's not your M.O. and second, I think you know my pretty red ass ain't selling niggas shit but dreams," Lucy said with conviction.

I checked her out and just looking at her, I would never have guessed her to be a scammer but then again how does a scammer look? Lucy was about 5'9, redbone, slim with fire red hair. She wasn't outrageously pretty but she was far from ugly. Lucy had this air about her though that made her appealing.

"Look, they say you're the best at what you do and I want you on my team. You're not going to be in the trenches or anything. All I'm going to need you to do is play with your computer."

"Say no more. I gotta request though," she grinned

"What?"

"I wanna be a part of Jackgirl Mafia, not JBM." She smirked.

I laughed. "Okay, bet. What's up with Ol' boy?" I nodded in the direction of her homeboy.

"Sheem is my homeboy. He thinks he's my bodyguard and the other people are just tag-alongs."

"Here, call this number and tell her what's up. You don't need a bodyguard anymore either. We take care of our own." I got up.

"Well, I'm getting some trouble with these niggas from Strickland Bridge Road."

"Give me their names and I'll handle it."

"Lil Rob and Deandre," she said the names of some of my little niggas.

"Don't sweat it, them my niggas"

I walked out of *Bottoms Up* with a smile on my face. I was about to fuck the game all the way up.

***

"I thought you had forgot about a real nigga," Ox said, letting me in the split level.

"Yea, right! Shit been wicked lately. What? Your pockets looking funny or something?" I questioned.

"Nah, I'm still sitting lovely. While you playing, the whole TNT is still sitting good," Ox bragged.

"Good. I'm gon' have some work for y'all to put in real soon. These ain't no regular joes. They're going to be hardened killers."

"We hardened killers too! I'm mad that you took my two youngins too," Ox joked, referring to Ogun and Oshun.

"Took them? They took me! I can't get rid of them. You might as well say they moved in with me." I sat down in the living room.

"Yo, what's the deal with Ross?" Ox's face darkened.

I looked at Ox. I hadn't told him about Ross's treachery so I didn't know what he was getting at.

"Not shit, he cooling to my understanding. Why? What's up?" I wanted to pick his brain.

"This mc, bra. Everybody knows he a slime ball and that he flipped sides on you. My question is, why haven't you let us punch his time card yet? Ox took a swig of the *Corona* he had in his hand.

I was stuck between a rock and a hard place. On the one hand, I wanted him dead in the worst way but on the other hand, I still had a certain amount of love for him, as much sense as that made. I knew I should only feel hate for the nigga but it was what it was.

"It's complicated but best believe he gon' get his. It's only a matter of time," I said confidently.

"We here if you need us. Use us."

"In due time, bra, in due time."

Chapter Twenty-Five

Just as I had wanted and expected, when the Colombians found their spot hit with some dead Sinaloa Cartel inside, they immediately took action. They hit a Mexican cartel dope house and killed everyone inside. It was no secret that the Sinaloa Cartel and the Medellin Cartel had set up shop in Fayetteville and were vying territory. So, bad blood had already been brewing before the recent killings but that sent them over the edge. Now they were going back and forth at a rapid pace. Now I was about to send a message to the underworld round table that Face wasn't the one to disrespect, nor was Fayetteville the spot to come to set up any kind of shop if you were an out-of-towner. And most definitely, don't piss of the baby mama of a young, fly, rich retarded nigga because Angie was playing a major roll in the demise of Alvaro Calderon.

I had scoped out the mansion that Alvaro had moved into and his security was everything I imagined it would be for the head of the Medellin Cartel. He spared no expense when it came to his security. The mansion was on a five-acre piece of land similar to the one me and Angie lived in but Alvaro's was enclosed in a white brick wall with cameras mounted all around it. Then he had pressure sensors all through the property and into the wood line. Also, he had ten guards scattered about that weren't as threatening as the three Bull Mastiffs that roamed about. But being that the security company he used was in Fayetteville, the only thing that I had to worry about was his armed guards and the dogs. Murph was fucking one of the bitches that worked for the alarm company, so the alarm system was a non-factor. Alvaro wasn't your run-of-the-mill hustler; he was the plug *plug*! So I wasn't going to be able to just kick his front door in. That would only lead to an early exit from the game. That was where Angie was going to come in. She was going to serve me her step dad up on a silver platter with a red apple in his mouth. I had planned it to where Angie was going to get us past the guards and into the house. Once inside me, Murph and Maino could handle the rest.

"Y'all need to hurry up. He's expecting me at 4 o'clock!" Angie yelled into the phone.

"Angie, shut up! We on the way right now." I hung up.

"Trouble on the home front?" Murph laughed.

"Fuck you! I don't know what kind of time Angie been on lately but she been on one. She been biting my head off for every little thing."

"Postpartum. She'll get over it sooner or later," Maino said.

"She better because it's starting to get on my last fucking nerve."

"You can talk to Dr. Phil later on," Murph chimed in.

"Maybe you niggas forgot but we're on the way to hit the head of the Medellin Cartel. Get y'all mind right! If shit don't go right, he'll have us and our entire family wiped off the face of the earth!" Murph continued.

"You smell that, Maino?" I asked.

"What are you talking about?"

"I don't know if it's fear or pussy I smell but it's coming from the passenger seat." I looked over at Murph.

"Fear? Nigga, you think I'd be dressed like this if I knew what fear of being a pussy was? Matter of fact, nigga, when we get done, you know what time it is." Murph started wolfing me.

"Nigga! Just because we got on all this gear don't mean a nigga can't be scared. Everybody fears something," Maino said.

"Everybody but me!" Murph screamed.

"Whateva you say," Maino smirked.

I pulled into Angie's driveway and she was sitting inside the Escalade I'd just bought for her. I parked and we loaded into the back.

"It took y'all long enough," she snapped.

"Blame your baby daddy," Murph added gas to the fire.

"He always doing some extra shit," she continued.

"Ang, shut all that stupid ass shit the fuck up!" I gritted my teeth and she rolled her eyes but didn't comment. She knew when I was serious.

"I'm going to be able to drive right in and into the garage. After that, it's on y'all to handle y'alls business and I don't think I need to remind y'all of the ramifications of not succeeding!" Angie warned.

"And what are they?" Maino questioned.

Angie looked in the rear-view mirror at him and said, "Death." The rest of the ride was quiet. We had never hit anybody of Alvaro's caliber. To mess up would most definitely mean death; not just for us, but our families as well. I didn't know about anybody else but I wasn't ready to die just yet.

"Get on the floor," Angie said as we got closer to Alvaro's.

The guards let us drive by the gate without so much as a glance inside the truck. So far so good. Angie drove into the garage and parked.

"Wait about five minutes then do what you do," Angie said and got out.

"Whose sting is this? Yours or hers?" Maino asked but I could hear the smile in his voice.

I ignored the question and said: "Look, shoot first and second, don't ask no questions. I don't want to leave here with anybody breathing but us."

"This my kind of party," Maino said.

Nicholas Lock

"Let's find out then." I hopped out the truck and ran inside the mansion.

My destination was to find Angie and Alvaro because I knew if I could get my hands on Alvaro, his soldiers would stand down.

Kah! Kah! Kah! I heard either Murph's or Maino's assault rifle crack.

I knew time was of the essence now! I started going inside every room I came across. *Bllt! Bllt! Bllt!* I let the Uzi in my hand spit three rounds into the chest of the Colombian rushing my way. I ran down the hall and into a room where I found Alvaro, Domonick, and Angie.

What I saw caused my heart to fall to my stomach.

"I didn't survive in this gang this long by being unaware or stupid," Alvaro said smugly from behind his desk.

"Domonick, the best decision you can make right now is to take that gun off Angie." I totally ignored Alvaro and his statement.

"You're worried about that whore when you need to be worried about how I'm going to make you and your family a distant memory!" Alvaro threatened.

I continued to ignore Alvaro because my focus was on Angie and the gun Domonick had against the side of her head. The fear in Angie's eyes had me unnerved. My sole focus was to get her out of harm's way, nothing else mattered.

"You think I didn't see the hatred in Angie's eyes? Her mother couldn't hide her frustrations either."

"Leave my mother out of this!" Angie screamed, catching us off guard because she had been quiet the entire time.

Then Murph and Maino burst into the room. When Domonick's eyes shifted to the two, I sent a round into his side and he dropped the gun he had on Angie. Before I could get a

134

chance to squeeze again, he hopped out of the window! I ran over to the window and Domonick was nowhere to be found!

"Your son left you to the wolves, Alvaro," I said, turning around and facing him.

"Psst!" Alvaro waved his hand as if to brush off what I said.

"That's the same way I feel. Now let's get down to why we're here. Where is the work and the money?"

"Work? Money?" He chuckled and spat. "I have fields of work and I have too much damn money. Is that all you want? What about power?" He grinned.

Kah! Kah! Maino let off two shots into the ceiling.

"Fuck all that, where is the work and money at? We don't have time for your riddles." Maino's face darkened.

"In Colombia," Alvaro grinned.

I waved Angie over. She had been standing off to the side. She was looking at me as if to say, *What?* I put the Uzi in her hand and stepped back. Angie looked down at the gun in her hands and up at Alvaro. I could see the hatred and fury in her eyes as she looked at him. Angie slowly pointed the gun at Alvaro and let it spit. She squeezed until the clip was empty.

"You let her kill the nigga, bra, and I'm cool with that but couldn't you have let him say what we needed to know first? I'm not about to search this big ass house," Murph's voice betrayed his frustration.

"Quit bitching," Angie said and walked behind Alvaro's desk.

Angie reached under Alvaro's desk and hit a switch. Alvaro's desk slid forward about three feet, revealing a trapdoor.

"That's where all the real work and money is. With the war going on between them and the Mexicans, Alvaro didn't want to risk losing any more money or product so he had all the excess moved here." Angie walked into my arms and put her head on my chest. I wrapped my arms around her as Murph and Maino went down the trapdoor.

"What's up?" I looked down at her trembling.

"Nothing. I just want to go get my baby and go home," she said into my chest.

"Bra, you need to peep this!" Murph yelled from the trapdoor.

"Go ahead home and I'll be there soon."

"Okay," she squeezed me and walked out.

I watched Angie walk away before going down the trapdoor.

"Oh shit!" I said in shock.

The trapdoor led me into a room that was about the size of two bedrooms. On one side of the room there were bricks from the floor to the ceiling and on the other side there were bundles of money stacked the same way as the bricks. The first word to come to my mind was *retirement*.

Chapter Twenty-Six

"Let's get this shit and get the fuck out of here," Maino said, already pulling money down.

"I'm gon' go pull their Navigator around to the front." I climbed the trapdoor and made my way to the garage. It was eerily quiet in the huge mansion. I got the keys to the Nav and ran to the garage. Took the seats out the back and pulled around to the front. I hopped out and opened the back so we could start loading everything in when a huge black bull Mastiff crept up to my right side. I saw him out of the corner of my eye. I turned to face him and he started growling. I eased my hand towards my hip where I had a Glock .23 then two more bull Mastiffs walked up growling, showing their teeth. I don't know how the fuck I had forgot about the dogs! I knew I could kill one of them but the other two were going to create an issue. *Kah! Kah! Kah! Kah! Kah!* The dogs got gunned down; I turned to see Murph standing off to the side smiling.

"Where would you be without me?"

"In a better place, now come on." I was ready to get the fuck away from Alvaro's.

I had shot Domonick before he was able to hop out of the window but I wasn't sure if the wound was a fatal one or not. In a perfect world, he would be laying in the woods dead but I knew than to hang my hope on that. We loaded up the SUV and got low. All I could do was smile because we had just hit the head of one of the deadliest, if not the deadliest, cartels known to man and got away with it. Life was good!

***

"If y'all want to keep robbing, I got you but I'm done with it and so is Chell. I'm done as far as physically taking part but

I'll still be behind the scenes," I informed every one of my decision.

I had everyone gathered at *Pleasure's Paradise.* My whole team was there: JGM, JBM, and TNT.

"Does Rai'chell know about this?" Sidney questioned.

I had purposely sent Chell on an errand so she wouldn't be in attendance. We had kinda talked about her falling back but hadn't made it official.

"Why wouldn't she? We stay in the same house, don't we?"

"Chell has a say-so in just about every decision I make." I quieted her down with my lie.

"Any more questions?" I asked.

"What about TNT? If you're done jacking niggas, then you know you're not gon' be terrorizing niggas," Ox said, fearing the worst.

"That don't mean it ain't gon' be niggas that need to be terrorized," I smiled, "but terrorizing niggas just because should no longer be a part of your agenda. We don't want or need any unwanted attention. For the most part, everything is the same. Maino still gon' be running JBM but as for JGM, Sidney is going to take Chell's place as the head of Jackgirl Mafia." I was taking Chell all the way out of the fold.

"I took care of *that* too," Lucy spoke up, causing everyone to look her way.

"For those of you who haven't met Lucy, she's the newest member of JGM. Lucy represents the new age of robbing. Lucy here is the best thing smoking when it comes to the scam game. She's the reason why everyone in this room is two point five million dollars richer. So it shouldn't be anyone here with money issues anytime soon," I let them know.

Alvaro had the info to one of his bank accounts on his desk the day we hit his house. Of course, I had Lucy hit Alvaro's bank account and empty it out. It couldn't have been his main one because the amount he had in it wasn't what I would've expected. There was still a nice chunk of change in it. I was able to put money in everybody's account and put a bunch away so that anybody on the team who got in trouble would have bond and lawyer money.

"Spend it wisely," I told them and dipped out.

I wasn't about to sit around for long. I had other loose ends that needed tying up.

"Where you at?" I asked Laci.

"At my house waiting on you," she said sexily.

"I'll be there in about fifteen minutes." I ended the call.

I had to pull up on Laci for a number of reasons, the main one being that before she left out after delivering me Pocahontas, that she said we needed to discuss *our* future. Now I'm pretty sure Laci knew that me and Chell were going strong so *our* future consisted of just what it was right now: friends with benefits. Laci was my little sneaky link.

I pulled up to Laci's spot and got out. She opened the door before I could knock. All I could do was shake my head. Since going to see Dr. Miami, Laci loved wearing the least amount of clothes possible. All she had on at the moment was a pair of lace boy shorts with the matching bra. I followed her to her bedroom and leaned up against her dresser while she sat on the edge of her California king.

"Why you way over there?" Laci scrunched her face up.

"What's up with this discussing our future shit?" I folded my arms.

"What do it sound like? We should be together. I thought I proved that. What other bitch has your back like me?!"

Laci started getting worked up. "I'm the bitch that put her freedom on the line so you could have your freedom. I'm the one who tracked that bitch Pocahontas down when I heard what she did! Don't I get any credit for any of that?" She paced back and forth.

"Hell yea, That's why you can quit your job and go pick you a house out. I got you as long as I got breath in my body but kill the *our future* talk. We don't even speak in that type of way. Besides, you know Chell is the wifey." I laid it out for her.

"So all this was for naught?" She waved her hand over her body. "I did this for you! You at least need to give us a chance," Laci pleaded.

"No, bitch! What he needs to do is get the fuck out of here and take his ass home!" Chell fumed.

Both me and Laci's head snapped towards her doorway. I don't know how they had gotten in Laci's apartment but the entire Jackgirl crew was standing in the doorway to Laci's bedroom with Rai'chell in the front.

"Y'all need to get the fuck out of my shit! And bitch! If you was taking care of home instead of running around in the streets, he probably wouldn't be here!" Laci snapped her neck.

Oh, boy! I thought to myself.

"Look, come on, Chell." I tried to grab her arm and she snatched away.

"Don't fucking touch me!" she glared at me then looked back at Laci.

"See, Face! I'd never tell you that. She don't deserve a nigga like you." Laci stood up

Before I could interject, Chell spoke up.

"See, I was just gonna beat yo' ass but since you got all that goddamn mouth I got something for you. Come here, Lucy."

"Hell no!" I said when Chell pulled her gun and handed it to Lacy.

"She need to earn her stripes," Chell said.

I stepped in front of Laci and said, "Y'all go ahead and get the fuck out of here. That shit ain't about nothing!"

Click! Click! A gun cocked behind me. I turned to see Laci holding a chrome .380.

"What the fuck are you doing, Laci? Chill, I got this," I said.

"Obviously, you don't! These bitches are still in my shit!"

Boom! Boom! Laci fell back on her bed with a crater in her face. I turned to see Desire holding a smoking gun.

"Y'all some stupid ass hoes!" I snapped and brushed past them.

Laci didn't deserve to die like that. I felt like it was my fault. I should've took care of her the way she took care of me but what could I do about it now?

Nicholas Lock

Chapter Twenty-Seven

"Listen, Face, my investigation on the Elite is about to come to a close and I purposely left you out of my report," Tasha informed me.

"That's why you had me drive way down here? You could've told me that over the phone, woman." I shook my head. I was sitting on Tasha's couch at her condo looking at her like she was crazy. I was in the process of trying to line Chino's ass up. I ain't have time to be dealing with Tasha's CIA ass.

"That's only part of the reason I called you over. You act as if you have something else better to do." Tasha walked over to where I was, handing me a glass of wine.

"What? I do! As do you. I see you're dressed for work." Tasha had on a black and gray YSL blouse, a black YSL skirt and some gray Chanel pumps.

"I called off after I got dressed. I ain't feeling it today." She continued standing in front of me.

"What are you feeling?"

"You," Tasha said, straddling my lap.

I hadn't been getting any pussy over the last week and a half because Chell was still on one about Laci, and Angie had been distant since killing Alvaro, so I was backed up sexually.

"When did these feelings come about?" I ran my hands up the sides of her thighs.

"Shh!" Tasha put her finger across my lips. "I don't want to talk. I want to get fucked."

"Say no more."

I lifted Tasha up and carried her to the bedroom. I sat her down on the edge of the bed and stepped back. I was here for one reason and one reason only: to fuck her brains out. I stripped down to my birthday suit while Tasha watched me. I stepped back up to her with my dick on ten. Tasha didn't need to be told what to do; she immediately took me into her mouth.

"Sss!" I grabbed two handfuls of Tasha's lace front and started fucking her mouth.

I was expecting Tasha to make me stop but she grabbed my hips and began pulling me deeper.

"Eat this dick then!"

I was pushing into her mouth with so much force that I was causing her head to snap back.

"Fuck!" I released my unborns into her mouth and she swallowed every drop. "Turn over."

Tasha got in the middle of the bed on her hands and knees and looked back at me. I got up on the bed and pulled her skirt up over her ass.

"Face!" Tasha yelped as I snatched off the G-string she was wearing.

"Shut that shit up," I said, lining my still hard member up with her love tunnel.

I went in Tasha slow while holding on to her wide hips.

"Ughh!" Tasha moaned and rocked back into me.

Tasha's pussy was grade A! It was tight and gushy. Seeing Tasha's sex cream covering my dick caused me to speed up and lengthen my strokes. While I sped up, she started squeezing me with her pussy muscles.

"Grr!" I growled, grabbing two handfuls of her ass. I was trying not to nut before Tasha but her pussy was doing something foreign to me. Tasha reached back between her legs and started massaging my balls. That set me off! I coated Tasha's walls with more of my kids and laid back on the bed spent. I looked over at Tasha and she was laying there staring at me.

"What are you looking at?" I questioned.

"Your young, non-fucking ass," she rolled her eyes.

"What!"

144

I got up and got between her legs. Tasha didn't have to be told; she put her thick legs on my shoulders.

"Nah, fuck all that." I pushed both her legs up until her feet was above her head, and slid all the way in.

I was pulling all the way out and slamming back into Tasha with so much force the mattress was starting to slide.

"Oh fuck! Fuck this pussy!" Tasha yelled as her eyes rolled into the back of her head.

I fucked Tasha at the same pace until her whole body started to shake and she gushed all over my dick.

"With my non-fucking ass," I said, looking down at her pretty red ass.

"Shut up," she grinned with her eyes closed.

I pulled out, got up and put my clothes on. By the time I got fully dressed, Tasha was curled up snoring lightly. I locked her door and let myself out of her condo. I had a Mexican to kill.

***

"You said you was on my side. It's time for you to prove it. How can I get to Chino?" I asked Lauren.

Lauren had previously told me that if push came to shove, she was going to take my side over Chino's.

"It took you long enough to ask. I've been lining shit up waiting on you to tell me you were ready," Lauren told me.

"Well, give me the rundown. What needs to be done?"

Lauren looked at me and smiled, causing her chinky eyes to narrow to slits.

"All you have to do is relax and I'm going to walk him to you but you have to give me Ross's spots and make sure they're immune to being robbed."

"His spots are yours but how am I supposed to make them immune to being robbed." I looked at her quizzically.

Lauren looked at me with a *'nigga, please'* look and said, "Tell your crew that my spots are off limits"

"Done," I said quickly.

"Give me a few hours and I'm going to call you with directions." She stood up and walked out of the Waffle House.

I had time to burn, so I was just about to cruise around the city. I got up and walked out of the Waffle House and Ogun, Oshun and Rai'chell were waiting on me with worried looks.

"What up? Why y'all looking like that?"

"Murph is down bad; it's all over the news," Chell said.

"What the fuck you mean?" I asked and she handed me her iPhone.

On her phone was a live shot from above Murph's mom's house with a million police officers surrounding it. I cut the volume up on the phone and the reporter said: "We're coming to you live from Ashton Forrest where the suspect from the Remington murders has barricaded himself inside this residential home."

Remington murders? I questioned, then the reporter gave me my answer.

"Apparently the suspect was injured and left his DNA on the scene—"

"Fuck!" I yelled.

Murph had gotten grazed inside the house in Remington that day we hit the Colombians. I called Murph's phone and he picked up on the first ring.

"I'm not going to prison, bro," were the first words he said.

"I got you, bro, just chill. Don't do nothing stupid. I can get you out of this." I tried reassuring him.

"Nah, brodie, I think they got me this time," he said dejectedly.

146

"Murph! Trust me, I got you, I got some people that can get you out of this."

"Face, I'm good, bro. I'm about to put the city on. They're gonna remember me forever. Love you, bro," he said and the line went dead.

I tried calling him back and it went straight to the voicemail.

"What he say?" Chell asked.

I didn't respond. I looked back down at the phone as a wave of police officers stormed the front door. Before they could get in the house, Murph started shooting, dropping two of them and forcing the others to run back for cover. Murph wasn't done! He opened the door with a Gatling gun in hand and opened fire!

Doon! Doon! Doon! The Gatling gun was spitting so many rounds at such a rapid pace that the police were forced to take cover.

"Eat, boy!" I yelled at the phone.

Murph shot all the cop cars up and a few of the police then ducked back inside. I was proud of my nigga; he was going out with a bang. But at the same time, I knew that the ending wasn't going to be in his favor. And what was eating at me the most was that there was really nothing I could do.

"What are you trying to do?" Oshun asked me as if she could read my mind.

"It's really nothing we can do besides go out with a bang with him," I shook my head.

"Look! Look!" Ogun pointed at the phone.

I looked and Murph came out of the house with a RPG gun and fired, blowing up two police cruisers. Before, the police were only taking cover but after Murph ducked back inside, they just started shooting the house up. Then the SWAT team showed up. They tried getting Murph to surrender but he was having none of it. They waited about an hour before they stormed the house again, only this time they got inside the house, which I assumed was Murph's plan. Because once all of the police got inside, the house exploded and fell in on itself.

"Oh my God!" Chell put her hand over her mouth.

My bro had gone out the way he wanted to, but that didn't lessen the hurt I was feeling. I allowed a single tear to run down my face before wiping it away. My phone chimed, alerting me that I had a text message. It was an address from Lauren.

"Ogun, Oshun, let's go. We're about to end this shit."

This was going to allow me to release this anger that was welled up in my chest.

Chapter Twenty-Eight

Me, Ogun and Oshun got in my Charger and rode off. Rai'chell must've known I wasn't going to allow her to come because she hopped in her truck and left. I put the address in the GPS as we rode down Raeford Road. The GPS said we were going to the condos downtown off of Hay Street. The same condos that Ross had a spot in. Tee Grizzley's "Satish" was playing while we rode. One of the things I loved the most about Ogun and Oshun is how they didn't ask any questions when it was time to ride out. Since getting in the car, they hadn't said a word. The only thing Oshun had been doing was playing with her knives. We pulled into the condos and got out.

"We're about to take Chino out the game," I told them while we were walking. I texted Lauren and told her I was outside the door.

"It's open" was her reply.

I pulled my Glock .29 out and eased the door open. I could hear talking coming from the living room and Chino's voice was one of them. I ran in the living room and saw Chino, Lauren, and Karla sitting in Chino's lap. I rushed over to Chino and put the Glock in his face.

"If you so much as blink wrong, I'm gon' put your thoughts all over this expensive ass Persian rug."

Karla looked at me with venom in her eyes and I slapped her off of his lap.

"Bitch, act like you know that I'll kill you in here!" I mugged her.

Clap, clap, clap. Chino clapped his hands together. "Bravo, I knew you had it in you all along, I just had to bring it out of you. Now I know you're ready for the position of power I have for you. All you have—"

Boom! Boom! I sent two hollow points in Chino's mouth, stopping him mid-sentence.

"Oh my God! What did you do?" Karla screamed, rushing over to Chino.

I looked over at Lauren and she just shrugged. Ogun and Oshun were looking at Lauren and Karla, hoping they made the wrong move. They weren't quite aware of the understanding that me and Lauren had.

"Come on, let's go," I said to Ogun and Oshun.

"Die, motherfucker!" Karla yelled and pointed a gun my way.

Boom! Lauren shot Karla and stood over her, shaking her head. I could see the tears brimming her eyes. *Boom!* Lauren dome-checked Karla, sending her to reunite with Chino.

"Blood makes us related but loyalty makes us family."

Lauren croaked, looking me in the eyes.

I nodded and walked out with Ogun and Oshun following close behind me. Lauren had just proved her loyalty to me. She was one person I knew had my back.

"I like her," Oshun said once we got in the car.

"Me too," I agreed.

"Oooh, you better not let Rai'chell hear you say that," Ogun added from the backseat.

"And you better not tell her," I warned.

"Never," he reassured me.

"Face, I need to talk to you about something but before I do I want to make sure I'm right," Oshun said softly.

"A'ight, just holla at me"

"Where are we going now?" Ogun questioned.

"We not going nowhere but hold that thought," I told him as my phone rang. "What up, Maino?"

"Where the hell is G'd-up and Abdullah at?" I been calling these niggas so they can hit this lick but they M.I.A," Maino said.

I started laughing. "Nigga, you know how they do, they probably laid up with some hoes somewhere but check it, I'm over here by Abdullah's crib right now so I'll swing by there and see if he home or not."

"If he is, tell him I'm looking for him."

"I got you," I said and ended the call. "After I drive by Abdullah's, I'm dropping y'all asses off. All my issues have been dealt with so I don't need y'all tagging along with me."

Oshun just looked at me but Ogun said, "I'm still going with you."

I pulled up to Abdullah's house in the good part of Haymount Hill and parked. Abdullah and G'd-up were sitting in G'd up's Tahoe in the driveway. I got out and walked up to the truck and tapped on the glass. G'd-up's playful ass didn't roll the window down; he just sat there so I snatched the door open.

"Oh shit!" I jumped back.

G'd-up and Abdullah's throats had been cut from ear to ear and their tongues had been pulled out through their necks. I immediately pulled my hammer out and started looking around. Sensing my mood Ogun and Oshun hopped out of the truck with their weapons at the ready. The way G'd-up and Abdullah had gotten killed was called a *Colombian necktie*. It earned that name because with the tongue pulled out through the neck it resembles a necktie. It was a signature of the cartels in Colombia. There was nothing that I could do for G'd-up and Abdullah, so I got back in the truck and called Maino. He didn't answer, so I hit him again and he still didn't answer. My mind was starting to think the worst but I knew Maino was too cautious to get caught lacking. I broke the speed limit all the way to Maino's house across the river. The minute I turned on Maino's street, I saw cop cars everywhere! They had the street blocked off, so I had to get out and walk.

"Y'all chill, I'll be right back," I told Ogun and Oshun.

I walked down the street towards Maino's house and all I saw were body bags littering his front yard. I just hoped none of them were Maino. I got to the edge of the crime scene tape and counted the body bags; there were eleven in all. Then I overheard two of the police talking amongst themselves saying how the homeowner took out ten intruders but died on the way to the hospital.

I was sick!

As the coroner was loading one of the body bags inside their van, it opened revealing a Colombian. I was under the assumption that I had dealt with all the Colombians when Angie had killed Alvaro but then it hit me like a .357 slug ... Domonick.

Chapter Twenty-Nine

Hoping Domonick had died from his wounds didn't pan out. Now with his dad dead, he was the head of the Medellin Cartel. And I knew it was going to take pure luck for me to get close to him again. I didn't know for a fact that Domonick was calling the shots because I hadn't seen him but it was no coincidence that a Colombian necktie had been used on G'd-up and Abdullah. Then a bunch of Colombians had ran in Maino's crib. I wasn't the smartest motherfucker in the world but I definitely wasn't the dumbest. They had wiped out the whole Jackboy Mafia in one day. All that was left was the Jackgirl Mafia! I had dropped Ogun and Oshun off because I had to go check on Angie and get some intel on Domonick. When I walked in the house Angie was breastfeeding my daughter. I sat across from her on the couch and asked, "What all can you tell me about Domonick?"

The minute my daughter heard my voice, she started trying to find me with her eyes.

"Hey, *how are you doing today*, would be nice," Angie replied while handing me Angelique.

"I ain't ask you all that and in case you haven't heard, the Medellin Cartel is out for blood. They took the remaining JBM out in a few hours. And I'm pretty sure they know the role you played in Alvaro's demise." I warned and her eyes got big.

"So you think Domonick is in charge now?"

"It has to be him," I answered while burping Angelique.

"Well, he's way worse than his father as far as temperament. So if he's alive he's not going to stop until everyone involved is dead," she shivered.

I got up and sat down beside her.

"You know I got you, baby. I'm not gon' let nothing happen to you or my baby girl."

"Okay." Angie lay her head on my shoulder.

We stayed like that until I heard her snoring softly. I looked down at my daughter and she was wide awake, looking up at me, blowing spit bubbles. I got up and let Angie lay down on the couch.

"You coming with daddy," I said and Angelique started smiling, showing me her gums.

I grabbed her diaper bag and put her in her car seat. I put her in the back of my Yukon and pulled out. I had a meeting with JGM and TNT. We had to put our heads together and come up with a plan to deal with Domonick. I pulled into *Pleasure's Paradise* and parked. Out of all my clubs Pleasure's Paradise was my favorite. It was probably because it was my first club, plus it had Cynthia's fingerprints all over it. I wonder how different my life would be had Cynthia not been killed. I probably would've been out of the streets, knowing how Cynthia was. I grabbed Angelique out the back and walked inside. Sidney had closed the club so that we could have our meeting but there were still dancers and bartenders milling about. The minute they saw Angelique, all of them rushed up to me trying to hold her. I let Fire grab Angelique while I went to meet everybody. I walked up the steps to the big VIP room where the entire TNT and JGM was. The mood was somber in the room.

"Everybody knows what happened earlier but what y'all don't know is who did it. Domonick is running the Medellin Cartel now. So the reason you're all here is because we need to come up with a plan to deal with him." I sat down beside Rai'chell.

"Let's just run up in his spot and do him in," one of the TNT members spoke up.

"Tell me where his spot is and we can do that," I said and he got quiet.

"What do we know about him? If you can get me some solid background information on him, I can track him down." Lucy gave me some hope because I didn't have an idea on how to proceed.

"Okay. I'm gon' get you that asap"

"What about Ross? He's long overdue for a meeting with the grim reaper."

"I got something special for him and that whole situation is personal, so I'm gon' be the one to handle it. So is everybody to the good?" I asked.

"Nah, I'm not good," a short light-skinned dude said.

He was a new recruit to TNT.

"You know what? I got something for you. Y'all trying to terrorize some shit?"

"Tali! Tali! Tali!" They started to chant in unison.

"A'ight. That spot in Taylors Creek that Ross got, rob it and burn it down." I gave them the go-ahead.

It was time to light a fire under Ross's ass. He'd been living without worry for long enough.

"What if Ross is there?" Ogun questioned.

"Call me but don't touch him," I said.

"What do you want us to do?" Marquita's pretty ass inquired.

"Y'all need some bread?" I wondered because I knew they should all be straight on the money tip.

"No, but we're bored. We need some action," Jasmine added.

"We do this robbing shit for fun," Desire chimed in.

"It's a sport," Rai'chell added.

"For them it might be but your ass knows better." I shut that shit down. "What y'all are saying is stupid as fuck but who am I to tell y'all what to do, so I got a few folders in the truck for y'all." I stood up signaling our meeting was over.

Rai'chell held me back as everyone filed out.

"Baby, I'm pregnant as fuck," she smiled.

"It's about time," I smiled with her.

"The only thing left to do is get married then our family will be complete," she threw me a hint.

"I got you, girl, just chill," I told her as we walked down the steps.

I grabbed my baby from Fire and we walked outside.

"I'ma give you some tonight, baby," Rai'chell said.

"Face, I need to speak to you," a voice said.

I turned to see Ryan Bush standing off to the side.

"Bae, take her to Angie." I hurried up and gave Rai'chell Angelique because I didn't know what type of time Ryan was on.

"You good?" Rai'chell asked, looking from me to Ryan.

I could tell by the look on her face that if I was to say no, she would try and up on him.

"Yea, now do what I said," I told her.

"I'm not about to take that woman her baby. I'ma just take her home with me. We'll be there when you get home," she said and got Angelique's car seat and put it in her Porsche.

"Come on," Ryan said, getting in the passenger seat of my truck.

"What brings you around these parts?" I asked, getting in the truck.

"Why does loyalty have an expiration date?" he asked.

"Huh?" I was lost.

"We're called the Elite for a reason. We're the top of the top. There's absolutely no one more powerful than us. The President of the United States can't compare to us. People would sell their soul to try and join us. Knowing all of that, it's still members who try and go against us."

"What are you getting at? I know you're not referring to me."

"Face, you know what I like about you? You don't abuse your power and you're not hungry for it. You're the exception because every other Elite wants to be in charge, even the Weeks. Yes, I know about the connection you have with them. Just like I know Tasha is an undercover CIA agent." Ryan's face darkened.

He had shocked me with his revelation about Tasha. His knowledge of the things he knew made me wonder what else he knew.

"If you know about Tasha, why is she still breathing?"

"What if I asked you the same thing, being that y'all have a personal relationship?" he asked suggestively.

I didn't really know how to respond, so I asked: "What are you going to do about it?"

"I'm not going to do shit. I'm going to leave her fate and yours up to you," he said and got out.

I got out to finish the conversation but by the time I got around to his side, he was getting in a black Audi. I rubbed my forehead in frustration because I had somehow got another problem dragged into my lap. And there was no mistaking the underlying threat in his words. One thing for certain: if a choice had to be made, it was going to be Tasha's funeral, not mine.

Nicholas Lock

Chapter Thirty

"Face, since we met, you've shown us nothing but love and loyalty so it's only right that we return the favor," Oshun said softly.

"What do y'all have up y'alls sleeve?" I asked the siblings.

"A murder scene." Ogun flashed a grin.

"I'm serious, boy." I laughed.

"I am too," he said, wiping the smile off my face. "Ox is a snake and we're about to take over TNT."

"Huh? Wait a minute, what I miss?" I questioned and Oshun spoke up.

"Face, it's dangerous to have a motherfucker around you that envies you. The whole time you looking at them like a friend but they're looking at you like an enemy."

"Where is this coming from?" I asked.

"Ox wants your position. He thinks he can lead better than you. After you sent us to burn Ross's trap down, Ox told us that if we caught Ross to kill him, fuck what you were talking about." Oshun laid it out.

"I think it started after Ox got out and we would go terrorize some shit and some of the TNT members would say Face didn't do it like that. He sees you as a threat to his position," Ogun chimed in.

I could only shake my head. It was like I was a magnet for disloyal ass niggas. I was the reason Ox even had his freedom and this is how he repays me. I could've let him rot in jail but I killed the victims in his case as soon as I went home. I hadn't been out a week. All so the D.A. wouldn't have a case.

"Don't worry about it, we got him. You just worry about trying to find Domonick." Oshun looked me directly in the eyes. It still amazed me that Oshun was as deadly as she was.

"Nah, Ox might be too much for y'all," I said because Ox got real retarded when the time called for it.

Oshun looked at me with that dead stare she had and said, "No such thing. We were born to get active, he had to learn." I nodded. I could tell she was dead set on her decision.

"What are y'all doing?" Rai'chell walked in the kitchen followed by Diqueena.

"Oh my God! Bro, I missed you." Diqueena wrapped me up in a hug.

"You don't fuck wit' me like that," I toyed with her.

"Don't do me like that!" she whined. "You know I fuck with you the long way. I know you thinking if I fuck with you why do I deal with Ross. I had to make sure I got to his bag first. Now tomorrow I'm going to lead him to you. Well, I'm going to give you the keycard to his penthouse and you do what you do."

"What penthouse?" I inquired because I didn't know anything about no penthouse.

He bought the penthouse at the top of the new condos that they just built off the boulevard.

"Say no more," I said, grabbing the keycard from her.

This was gonna be Karma for him. He'd sold me out and now he was about to get a dose of his own medicine. He was going to see what it felt like to be stabbed in the back by someone that you had love for.

"I'm gon' catch up to all later on. Ogun, Oshun, y'all be safe," I said and walked out of the house.

I got in the new Pepsi blue Corvette Z06 that Rai'chell had got me and burnt rubber. I really wanted to be by myself at the moment. I just couldn't understand how the ones you showed the most love to ended up being the first ones to betray you. I hadn't been gone from the house for ten minutes when my phone started blowing up.

"Yea," I answered.

"I know where Domonick is!" Lucy yelled in my ear.

"Where?"

"He's been right under our noses the entire time! He's staying in King's Grant; the address is 1321 Roundly Drive."

"Good shit, girl! I'll hit you up later." I ended the call.

Domonick had to know I would try and track him down. He had to be the dumbest criminal in the world, or him being the new head of the Medellin Cartel had him feeling untouchable. I was glad either way because he'd made my job that much easier. If he would've gone back to Colombia, I pretty much know I wouldn't have been able to touch him. I drove to the address Lucy gave me and rode by. For the most part, the house wasn't anything spectacular; it was just big as hell. It was a three-story white brick house. I couldn't spot any security but I knew for a fact that it was there. A house out in the open was actually a smart idea because no one would expect the leader of the Medellin Cartel not to be in a gated community. I wasn't prepared for him at the moment, so Domonick would get to live another day. Plus I didn't want to rush it; I didn't need him getting away again. One thing for sure though: This time, Domonick was going to meet the same fate as his pops.

***

"What's wrong, baby?" Chell asked.

I was standing in the window looking out, lost in my thoughts. I was trying to mentally prepare myself to kill Ross. The task wasn't going to be an easy one, even though he'd stabbed me in the back. I believed Karma was real, so you would get what you deserved, so I would be content to just allow Karma to catch up to him. But I also had a team that was watching my moves, so it was really impossible for me not to do anything. The message that would send isn't one that I wanted to send.

"Nothing, just thinking." I turned and sat on the bed beside her.

"Baby, I need you to be here for our baby." She grabbed my hand and put it on her ever growing stomach.

"I'm gon' be here, woman, you ain't gotta worry about that," I reassured her with a kiss.

"Good because I can't and won't live without you," Chell said seriously.

"Look, bae, I'm not going nowhere but hypothetically speaking, if something was to happen to me, I expect you to hold the fort down."

"I wouldn't be able to," her voice trembled.

I grabbed Rai'chell's face with both hands and forced her to look me in the eyes.

"Chell, everything gon' be okay whether I'm here or not. Suck that shit up." I leaned down and stuck my tongue in her mouth.

I could feel the love times ten every time we kissed and now was no different.

"I'll be back." I broke the kiss and walked out before she could try and stop me.

I took the keys to Chell's S550 and drove off. I got to Ross's condo before I knew it. I put one in the head of my Springfield .40 and got out. All the memories that me and Ross had shared were going through my mind as I rode the elevator up to the top floor. It was dead quiet when I stepped off the elevator. The way the condo was set up, the top floor had four penthouses suites, two on each side. I knew from Diqueena that Ross's was the last one on the left. I put the keycard in the door and slid in. I tiptoed through the suite until

I got to his bedroom. I peeked through the cracked door and saw Diqueena facing me, riding Ross. I was stuck at first but then I rushed in the room. Diqueena hopped up when I ran in the room.

"Damn, bra! What's going on?" Ross asked when he realized I was standing in the room.

"Bra? You ain't no brother of mine!" I glared at him.

Boom! I shot him in the stomach.

"Nigga, you turned on me! A nigga that shed blood and risked his life for you!" I yelled, my voice laced with pain.

Boom! I shot him in the arm.

"It ain't what you think! I was just rocking the nigga to sleep." Ross pleaded his case.

"Watch out, he's got a gun under the pillow," Diqueena warned me.

Boom! Boom! The hollow tips from the .40 caved the bottom of his face in. I walked over to the bed and flipped the pillow over and, sure enough, Ross had his hand on a Desert Eagle. I shook my head and walked out. That chapter of my life was closed; now it was time to end the book.

Chapter Thirty-One

I had been trying to get in contact with Tasha for the last couple of days and couldn't. I had even gone by her condo. I didn't even know what I was going to do or say upon talking to her. I really felt like Tasha was more Ryan's problem than mine.

"Baby, come here!" Chell yelled from downstairs.

I ran down the steps with my gun out thinking something was going on.

"Look! Look!" she pointed at the TV screen.

I looked and saw breaking news flashing across the screen: top officials arrested in raid. I turned the volume up just as the reporter came on.

"In a multi-government raid, several key members of Fayetteville's legal system were taken into custody, one of whom was the Mayor. The Chief of Police and Sheriff of Fayetteville were some of the other members taken into custody. Director of C.I.A William Kates said that the people taken into custody were a part of a secret organization called the Elite. They controlled and perverted the justice system in North Carolina. He also stated that this was just the tip of the iceberg and there were more arrests coming."

Tasha wasn't playing; she had taken down the Elite but she wouldn't get to bask in her accomplishments. She was officially a dead woman walking. All I could do was shake my head. *Damn!* I thought to myself. With her taking down the Elite, where did that leave me?" Who was going to take over? Would I still have immunity?"

"If all of them were crooked, how many people do you think they railroaded?" Chell asked.

"Too many to count," I said, thinking of how many dudes that were going to get back in court.

Bzz . . . bzzz! I looked down at my phone and saw Ox calling me.

"Yo," I answered.

"I'm in a good mood, so I ain't gone kill Oshun and Ogun but if you care about them you'll meet at the park in Hope Mills," Ox said.

"I'll be there in an hour," I said and hung up.

"Where are you about to go?" Chell asked.

"Call up the girls and tell them I said to meet me at the Wal-Mart on Hope Mills Road."

I went to the walk-in closet and grabbed my vest. I was mad as fuck! I had told them not to play no games with the nigga but obviously they hadn't listened. Now I was being forced to deal with Ox on his terms but I was going to make sure I had the upper hand.

"They said okay and I'm coming too," Chell told me.

"No, the fuck you not, you got a whole baby in your stomach!" I glared at her.

"Yes, the fuck I am!" she matched my tone.

"I'm really not in the mood for your shit, Chell!" I warned.

"At least let me drive you there," she pleaded softly.

"A'ight but put a fucking vest on," I said, loading some hollow tips into my twin H&K .40's.

Rai'chell put on a black light weight vest that looked like a coat and went to warm the car up. I went through my contacts and sent a few texts in an attempt to set the deck in my favor. I walked out of the house and got in the passenger seat beside Chell.

"Are you going to tell me what's going on?" Chell's nosey ass asked.

"Ox has Oshun and Ogun and basically wants me in exchange for them," I summed it up for her.

"No, the fuck you're not!" She slammed on brakes.

"Stop playing and drive!" I yelled, looking around. "You act like we're not riding dirty."

Chell started back driving and I leaned back in my seat.

"You ain't got to worry about me, baby girl, I'm good. I always got a trick up my sleeve," I tried easing her nerves.

"Okay but if shit starts looking shaky, I'm getting out," Chell said and the look she had on her face let me know it wouldn't do any good to argue.

When we pulled into the parking lot, the girls were already there. I got out and they followed suit. They must've knew some shit was about to go down because they were all dressed in camo pants and tops. Even Lucy was dressed for war. The Jackgirl Mafia was ready for whatever.

"Lucy, you can go, you already know you not to be in the trenches," I stated.

"No, stay. You're not about to be babying her, let her bust her gun," Chell protested.

"Whatever." I didn't feel like going back and forth with her. "Check it, Ox isn't on our side anymore. He has Ogun and Oshun and he wants me to come to Hope Mills park to ensure their safety. I just need y'all to watch my back because he's gunning for me," I informed them.

"Fuck him! I never liked him anyway," Tatianna's chocolate ass said.

"First one to put a bullet through his head gets a hundred bands," Chell said.

"You might as well pay me now," Sidney said, her green eyes filled with malice.

"Picture that," Desire added.

Marquita and Jasmine looked at each other and smirked. I knew they were probably thinking that they were going to be the ones to collect on Rai'chell's bounty. They had turned into real flame throwers since forming the Jackgirl Mafia.

"Lucy, you back them up, you know what your real role is. Leave the gun busting to the other girls," I said, getting back in the car.

We drove the short trip from the Wal-Mart to the park.

"Stay in the car, Chell, and I'm dead serious!" I warned her before I got out.

"Where you at? I'm out here," I called Ox.

"I see you. I'm over here on the basketball court," he said.

I ended the call and started making my way to the basketball court. Desire, Sidney and Lucy were on my left; and Marquita, Tatianna, and Jasmine were on my right. My temperature went on 1,000 when I saw Ogun and Oshun tied to one of the basketball goals.

"That's how you do the ones you fuck with?" I asked him but I was looking at the mob of Taliban members he had at his back.

There weren't any Tiaras in the group.

"Only those who betray me and mine!" he shot back, grilling me.

"Fuck talking! What are we doing because I got shit I need to do," Tatianna said, ready to blow smoke.

Ox laughed. "She funny as fuck, yo, but you might want to tell her to stay in a woman's place."

"You tell her, fuck nigga!" Marquita snapped.

"Chill real quick" I told them because I could see that they were on edge. "So what's up? You got me out here, so let Oshun and Ogun go."

"I'ma do that but me and you need to go head up, man to man since you're the reason they tried me.

Now it was my turn to laugh. "Head to head, huh? And are you sure I'm the reason they tried you or are you the real reason with your disloyal ass? Matter of fact, I'm done talking."

On cue the Tiaras walked on the court.

"Tiara gang! Tiara gang!" They yelled in unison.

Ox started pulling his gun and the Taliban member to his right grabbed his hand and put his gun under Ox's chin. I smiled at Ox as the Tiaras untied Oshun and Ogun.

"I'd hate to be you right now, bro. You see, loyalty is still high on some people's list. You may be disloyal but your team isn't and did you really think that tying Oshun and Ogun up to a basketball goal was going to sit right with everybody?" I flashed him a sarcastic grin.

"TNT is me and my brothers now. Your services are on longer needed," Oshun said, walking up to Ox.

Ogun was so mad I could see the steam coming off his young head. *Boom! Boom!* Ogun shot Ox in his legs, dropping him to his knees. So now him and Oshun were eye to eye. Instead of making Ox suffer, she just ran one of her knives across his throat. I didn't wait to see him bleed out; I walked away with the girls right behind me.

"You knew all them Taliban niggas was on your side the whole time?" Lucy said.

"Yea, I talked to them earlier." I smirked, getting in the car with Rai'chell.

"What happened? Who got the bounty?" Chell asked.

"Oshun. Now let's go. I need to relieve some stress." I leaned my seat back thinking to myself that everything was almost over.

Nicholas Lock

Chapter Thirty-Two

"Aye, cuz, it's this bitch over here trying to open up shop in Ross's old traps. She saying you gave her the go-ahead," Sha Loc said into the phone.

"What she look like?" I inquired.

"A tall, thick bitch with chinky eyes," Sha Loc described Lauren.

"Yea, yea, that's my people." I had forgot I had given Lauren the okay to open up Ross's old spots. "And I thought you had gave up the life."

"For the most part I did but I still dibble and dabble a little bit."

"So is she going to fuck up your thing?" I had to make sure her setting up shop wouldn't fuck up his cash flow.

"Nah, she straight. I just had to make sure she wasn't lying. And that's fucked up about Ross too," Sha Loc said but I could hear the smile in his voice. "We need to kick it, my nigga."

"I already know, Loc, but shit been so hectic. The first chance I get we gon' link up," I said.

"A'ight, bet." He hung up and I called Lauren.

"You ain't waste no time, did you?" I asked Lauren.

"Nope. It's a lot of money to be made and I plan on making it," she responded. "Are you straight though? Whenever you get ready to ride on anything, call me and I'm there."

"Sit down, woman, I got this on my end. You just make sure you come let a nigga blow your back out."

"I'm on the way right now."

"Hell no. I got something going on right now with your crazy ass." I laughed.

"Call me the minute you get done," Lauren said anxiously.

"Bye!" I ended the call, shaking my head.

I was about to ride past Domonick's spot one last time before I put the plan together to help him breathe his last few breaths.

As I was pulling into King's Grant, five Tahoes drove past me. Just my luck! I knew that the Tahoes were Domonick and his security. I was still going to drive past his house just to make sure I had the layout down.

"What the fuck!" I said out loud when I got by his house.

Domonick was pushing Angie into the house. By the time I hopped out the Vette, he had already closed the door. I took off full speed towards the house, drawing the XD .45 off my waist. I didn't slow down or break stride, I kicked the front door off of the hinges. Domonick spun around but before he could react, I shot him in the stomach, causing him to fall to the floor.

"Oh my God, baby! Thank God! I thought he was going to kill me." Angie rushed into my arms.

"You good, bae, I got you." I walked over to where Domonick was laying on the ground clutching his stomach.

"You killed the last of the people I had love for." I pointed the gun in his face.

"Let me do it, baby," Angie said.

Angie had killed Alvaro so why not let her kill his son too. I handed Angie the .45 and stepped back to let her work. Angie pointed the gun at Domonick then turned back my way and fired three times *Boom! Boom! Boom!* The .45 slugs hit me square in the chest and knocked me off my feet.

"Baby, are you okay?" Angie asked.

I turned on my side to see her crouching over Domonick. *Baby?* My head was spinning. I was confused. Angie helped Domonick sit up and looked back at me.

"Confused?" Angie asked. "Let me let you in on a secret. Remember when I told you that Alvaro sent me to the States because I had started rebelling. Well, the real reason he sent me off was because me and Domonick got caught having sex and were madly in love. I thought our love was over but when we saw each other for the first time after all those years, the feelings came back. And I knew that if you robbed Alvaro, that he wouldn't make it out of the situation alive and he was the only thing stopping me and Domonick's love. Plus with Alvaro out of the way, it would put my love in charge of the cartel. I'm still grateful for you, Face, because you helped me get off crack and gave me a beautiful daughter but my heart belongs to Domonick, sorry." Angie shrugged. "Come on, baby, so I can get you some help." She helped Domonick stand up and started helping him to the door.

My chest was burning up! I knew if I didn't get up, I was going to bleed to death.

Kah! Kah! Kah! Kah! I heard gunfire going off outside.

"Oh my God, bae!" Chell appeared above me. "Get up so we can get you to the hospital." She tried lifting me up.

"Chill, Chell, I'm hurting." I coughed up some blood.

"Come on, Face, we have to get you some help." Diqueena grabbed me on my other side.

They got me up and helped me to the backseat of Diqueena's S600. On the way to the car I saw Angie and Domonick side by side with bullet holes decorating their bodies.

"Don't close your eyes, baby!" Chell shook me awake.

"Wake me up when we get to the hospital," I said softly, closing my eyes again.

"No! Get up!" she yelled but it was too late. "Please don't leave me, baby. I need you!" Chell started getting hysterical.

"Get up, Face!" Diqueena cried, looking over the seat, seeing I was gone.

***

"I told you I couldn't live without you and I'm not going to." Rai'chell grabbed the gun.

"No, Chell!" Diqueena yelled, pulling the car over.

"No, Chell what?" Rai'chell asked, not bothering to look up from checking the clip.

"Don't do anything stupid"

"I'm not, you are." Chell put the gun on the middle console.

"What are you talking about?" Diqueena was utterly lost.

"Shoot me or I'ma shoot you. That's on Face."

Diqueena knew she was dead serious by saying it was on Face. She knew how much Chell loved him.

"Come on, so I can catch up to my baby." Chell rubbed her hand down Tymel's face.

"You got until the count of three," Chell said. "One—"

Boom! Diqueena shot Chell twice, sending her best friend to be with her soulmate.

The End

Confessions of a Jackboy 3

Lock Down Publications and Ca$h Presents assisted publishing packages.

BASIC PACKAGE $499
Editing
Cover Design
Formatting

UPGRADED PACKAGE $800
Typing
Editing
Cover Design
Formatting

ADVANCE PACKAGE $1,200
Typing
Editing
Cover Design
Formatting
Copyright registration
Proofreading
Upload book to Amazon

LDP SUPREME PACKAGE $1,500
Typing
Editing
Cover Design
Formatting
Copyright registration
Proofreading
Set up Amazon account
Upload book to Amazon

Nicholas Lock

Advertise on LDP Amazon and Facebook page

***Other services available upon request. Additional charges may apply
Lock Down Publications
P.O. Box 944
Stockbridge, GA 30281-9998
Phone # 470 303-9761

Submission Guideline

Submit the first three chapters of your completed manuscript to ldpsubmissions@gmail.com, subject line: Your book's title. The manuscript must be in a .doc file and sent as an attachment. Document should be in Times New Roman, double spaced and in size 12 font. Also, provide your synopsis and full contact information. If sending multiple submissions, they must each be in a separate email.

Have a story but no way to send it electronically? You can still submit to LDP/Ca$h Presents. Send in the first three chapters, written or typed, of your completed manuscript to:

LDP: Submissions Dept
Po Box 944
Stockbridge, Ga 30281

DO NOT send original manuscript. Must be a duplicate.

Provide your synopsis and a cover letter containing your full contact information.

Thanks for considering LDP and Ca$h Presents.

NEW RELEASES

THE BLACK DIAMOND CARTEL by SAYNOMORE

THE BIRTH OF A GANGSTER 3 by DELMONT
PLAYER

SALUTE MY SAVAGERY by FUMIYA PAYNE

THE COCAINE PRINCESS 10 by KING RIO

CONFESSIONS OF A JACKBOY 3 by NICHOLAS
LOCK

Nicholas Lock

By **T.J. Edwards**
GORILLAZ IN THE BAY V
3X KRAZY III
STRAIGHT BEAST MODE III
De'Kari
KINGPIN KILLAZ IV
STREET KINGS III
PAID IN BLOOD III
CARTEL KILLAZ IV
DOPE GODS III
Hood Rich
SINS OF A HUSTLA II
ASAD
YAYO V
Bred In The Game 2
S. Allen
THE STREETS WILL TALK II
By Yolanda Moore
SON OF A DOPE FIEND III
HEAVEN GOT A GHETTO III
SKI MASK MONEY III
By Renta
LOYALTY AIN'T PROMISED III
By Keith Williams
I'M NOTHING WITHOUT HIS LOVE II
SINS OF A THUG II
TO THE THUG I LOVED BEFORE II

IN A HUSTLER I TRUST II

By Monet Dragun

QUIET MONEY IV

EXTENDED CLIP III

THUG LIFE IV

By **Trai'Quan**

THE STREETS MADE ME IV

By **Larry D. Wright**

IF YOU CROSS ME ONCE III

ANGEL V

By **Anthony Fields**

THE STREETS WILL NEVER CLOSE IV

By K'ajji

HARD AND RUTHLESS III

KILLA KOUNTY IV

By Khufu

MONEY GAME III

By Smoove Dolla

JACK BOYS VS DOPE BOYS IV

A GANGSTA'S QUR'AN V

COKE GIRLZ II

COKE BOYS II

LIFE OF A SAVAGE V

CHI'RAQ GANGSTAS V

SOSA GANG IV

BRONX SAVAGES II

BODYMORE KINGPINS II

Nicholas Lock

BLOOD OF A GOON II
By Romell Tukes
MURDA WAS THE CASE III
Elijah R. Freeman
AN UNFORESEEN LOVE IV
BABY, I'M WINTERTIME COLD III
By **Meesha**

QUEEN OF THE ZOO III
By **Black Migo**
KING KILLA II
By Vincent "Vitto" Holloway
BETRAYAL OF A THUG III
By Fre$h
THE BIRTH OF A GANGSTER IV
By Delmont Player
TREAL LOVE II
By Le'Monica Jackson
FOR THE LOVE OF BLOOD IV
By Jamel Mitchell
RAN OFF ON DA PLUG II
By Paper Boi Rari
HOOD CONSIGLIERE III
By Keese
PRETTY GIRLS DO NASTY THINGS II
By Nicole Goosby
LOVE IN THE TRENCHES II

Confessions of a Jackboy 3

By Corey Robinson
FOREVER GANGSTA III
By Adrian Dulan
SUPER GREMLIN II
By King Rio
CRIME BOSS II
Playa Ray
LOYALTY IS EVERYTHING III
Molotti
HERE TODAY GONE TOMORROW II
By Fly Rock
REAL G'S MOVE IN SILENCE II
By Von Diesel
GRIMEY WAYS IV
By Ray Vinci
BLOOD AND GAMES II
By King Dream
THE BLACK DIAMOND CARTEL II
By SayNoMore

Available Now

Nicholas Lock

RESTRAINING ORDER **I & II**

By **CA$H & Coffee**

LOVE KNOWS NO BOUNDARIES **I II & III**

By **Coffee**

RAISED AS A GOON I, II, III & IV

BRED BY THE SLUMS I, II, III

BLAST FOR ME I & II

ROTTEN TO THE CORE I II III

A BRONX TALE I, II, III

DUFFLE BAG CARTEL I II III IV V VI

HEARTLESS GOON I II III IV V

A SAVAGE DOPEBOY I II

DRUG LORDS I II III

CUTTHROAT MAFIA I II

KING OF THE TRENCHES

By **Ghost**

LAY IT DOWN **I & II**

LAST OF A DYING BREED I II

BLOOD STAINS OF A SHOTTA I & II III

By **Jamaica**

LOYAL TO THE GAME I II III

LIFE OF SIN I, II III

By **TJ & Jelissa**

BLOODY COMMAS I & II

SKI MASK CARTEL I II & III

KING OF NEW YORK I II,III IV V

RISE TO POWER I II III

COKE KINGS I II III IV V
BORN HEARTLESS I II III IV
KING OF THE TRAP I II
By **T.J. Edwards**
IF LOVING HIM IS WRONG…I & II
LOVE ME EVEN WHEN IT HURTS I II III
By **Jelissa**
WHEN THE STREETS CLAP BACK I & II III
THE HEART OF A SAVAGE I II III IV
MONEY MAFIA I II
LOYAL TO THE SOIL I II III
By **Jibril Williams**
A DISTINGUISHED THUG STOLE MY HEART I II & III
LOVE SHOULDN'T HURT I II III IV
RENEGADE BOYS I II III IV
PAID IN KARMA I II III
SAVAGE STORMS I II III
AN UNFORESEEN LOVE I II III
BABY, I'M WINTERTIME COLD I II
By **Meesha**
A GANGSTER'S CODE I &, II III
A GANGSTER'S SYN I II III
THE SAVAGE LIFE I II III
CHAINED TO THE STREETS I II III
BLOOD ON THE MONEY I II III
A GANGSTA'S PAIN I II III
By **J-Blunt**

Nicholas Lock

PUSH IT TO THE LIMIT
By **Bre' Hayes**
BLOOD OF A BOSS **I, II, III, IV, V**
SHADOWS OF THE GAME
TRAP BASTARD
By **Askari**
THE STREETS BLEED MURDER **I, II & III**
THE HEART OF A GANGSTA I II& III
By **Jerry Jackson**
CUM FOR ME I II III IV V VI VII VIII
An **LDP Erotica Collaboration**
BRIDE OF A HUSTLA **I II & II**
THE FETTI GIRLS **I, II& III**
CORRUPTED BY A GANGSTA I, II III, IV
BLINDED BY HIS LOVE
THE PRICE YOU PAY FOR LOVE I, II ,III
DOPE GIRL MAGIC I II III
By **Destiny Skai**
WHEN A GOOD GIRL GOES BAD
By **Adrienne**
THE COST OF LOYALTY I II III
By Kweli
A GANGSTER'S REVENGE **I II III & IV**
THE BOSS MAN'S DAUGHTERS I II III IV V
A SAVAGE LOVE **I & II**
BAE BELONGS TO ME I II
A HUSTLER'S DECEIT I, II, III

186

WHAT BAD BITCHES DO I, II, III

SOUL OF A MONSTER I II III

KILL ZONE

A DOPE BOY'S QUEEN I II III

TIL DEATH

By **Aryanna**

A KINGPIN'S AMBITON

A KINGPIN'S AMBITION **II**

I MURDER FOR THE DOUGH

By **Ambitious**

TRUE SAVAGE I II III IV V VI VII

DOPE BOY MAGIC I, II, III

MIDNIGHT CARTEL I II III

CITY OF KINGZ I II

NIGHTMARE ON SILENT AVE

THE PLUG OF LIL MEXICO I II

CLASSIC CITY

By **Chris Green**

A DOPEBOY'S PRAYER

By **Eddie "Wolf" Lee**

THE KING CARTEL **I, II & III**

By **Frank Gresham**

THESE NIGGAS AIN'T LOYAL **I, II & III**

By **Nikki Tee**

GANGSTA SHYT **I II &III**

By **CATO**

THE ULTIMATE BETRAYAL

Nicholas Lock

By **Phoenix**

BOSS'N UP **I , II & III**

By **Royal Nicole**

I LOVE YOU TO DEATH

By **Destiny J**

I RIDE FOR MY HITTA

I STILL RIDE FOR MY HITTA

By **Misty Holt**

LOVE & CHASIN' PAPER

By **Qay Crockett**

TO DIE IN VAIN

SINS OF A HUSTLA

By **ASAD**

BROOKLYN HUSTLAZ

By **Boogsy Morina**

BROOKLYN ON LOCK I & II

By **Sonovia**

GANGSTA CITY

By **Teddy Duke**

A DRUG KING AND HIS DIAMOND I & II III

A DOPEMAN'S RICHES

HER MAN, MINE'S TOO I, II

CASH MONEY HO'S

THE WIFEY I USED TO BE I II

PRETTY GIRLS DO NASTY THINGS

By **Nicole Goosby**

TRAPHOUSE KING **I II & III**

KINGPIN KILLAZ I II III
STREET KINGS I II
PAID IN BLOOD **I II**
CARTEL KILLAZ I II III
DOPE GODS I II
By **Hood Rich**
LIPSTICK KILLAH **I, II, III**
CRIME OF PASSION I II & III
FRIEND OR FOE I II III
By **Mimi**
STEADY MOBBN' **I, II, III**
THE STREETS STAINED MY SOUL I II III
By **Marcellus Allen**
WHO SHOT YA **I, II, III**
SON OF A DOPE FIEND I II
HEAVEN GOT A GHETTO I II
SKI MASK MONEY I II
Renta
GORILLAZ IN THE BAY **I II III IV**
TEARS OF A GANGSTA I II
3X KRAZY I II
STRAIGHT BEAST MODE I II
DE'KARI
TRIGGADALE I II III
MURDAROBER WAS THE CASE I II
Elijah R. Freeman
GOD BLESS THE TRAPPERS I, II, III

Nicholas Lock

THESE SCANDALOUS STREETS I, II, III
FEAR MY GANGSTA I, II, III IV, V
THESE STREETS DON'T LOVE NOBODY I, II
BURY ME A G I, II, III, IV, V
A GANGSTA'S EMPIRE I, II, III, IV
THE DOPEMAN'S BODYGAURD I II
THE REALEST KILLAZ I II III
THE LAST OF THE OGS I II III
Tranay Adams
THE STREETS ARE CALLING
Duquie Wilson
MARRIED TO A BOSS I II III
By Destiny Skai & Chris Green
KINGZ OF THE GAME I II III IV V VI VII
CRIME BOSS
Playa Ray
SLAUGHTER GANG I II III
RUTHLESS HEART I II III
By Willie Slaughter
FUK SHYT
By Blakk Diamond
DON'T F#CK WITH MY HEART I II
By Linnea
ADDICTED TO THE DRAMA I II III
IN THE ARM OF HIS BOSS II
By Jamila
YAYO I II III IV

A SHOOTER'S AMBITION I II

BRED IN THE GAME

By S. Allen

TRAP GOD I II III

RICH $AVAGE I II III

MONEY IN THE GRAVE I II III

By Martell Troublesome Bolden

FOREVER GANGSTA I II

GLOCKS ON SATIN SHEETS I II

By Adrian Dulan

TOE TAGZ I II III IV

LEVELS TO THIS SHYT I II

IT'S JUST ME AND YOU I II

By Ah'Million

KINGPIN DREAMS I II III

RAN OFF ON DA PLUG

By Paper Boi Rari

CONFESSIONS OF A GANGSTA I II III IV

CONFESSIONS OF A JACKBOY I II III

By Nicholas Lock

I'M NOTHING WITHOUT HIS LOVE

SINS OF A THUG

TO THE THUG I LOVED BEFORE

A GANGSTA SAVED XMAS

IN A HUSTLER I TRUST

By Monet Dragun

CAUGHT UP IN THE LIFE I II III

Nicholas Lock

THE STREETS NEVER LET GO I II III
By Robert Baptiste
NEW TO THE GAME I II III
MONEY, MURDER & MEMORIES I II III
By **Malik D. Rice**
LIFE OF A SAVAGE I II III IV
A GANGSTA'S QUR'AN I II III IV
MURDA SEASON I II III
GANGLAND CARTEL I II III
CHI'RAQ GANGSTAS I II III IV
KILLERS ON ELM STREET I II III
JACK BOYZ N DA BRONX I II III
A DOPEBOY'S DREAM I II III
JACK BOYS VS DOPE BOYS I II III
COKE GIRLZ
COKE BOYS
SOSA GANG I II III
BRONX SAVAGES
BODYMORE KINGPINS
BLOOD OF A GOON
By Romell Tukes
LOYALTY AIN'T PROMISED I II
By Keith Williams
QUIET MONEY I II III
THUG LIFE I II III
EXTENDED CLIP I II
A GANGSTA'S PARADISE

By **Trai'Quan**

THE STREETS MADE ME I II III

By **Larry D. Wright**

THE ULTIMATE SACRIFICE I, II, III, IV, V, VI

KHADIFI

IF YOU CROSS ME ONCE I II

ANGEL I II III IV

IN THE BLINK OF AN EYE

By **Anthony Fields**

THE LIFE OF A HOOD STAR

By **Ca$h & Rashia Wilson**

THE STREETS WILL NEVER CLOSE I II III

By **K'ajji**

CREAM I II III

THE STREETS WILL TALK

By **Yolanda Moore**

NIGHTMARES OF A HUSTLA I II III

BLOOD AND GAMES

By **King Dream**

CONCRETE KILLA I II III

VICIOUS LOYALTY I II III

By **Kingpen**

HARD AND RUTHLESS I II

MOB TOWN 251

THE BILLIONAIRE BENTLEYS I II III

REAL G'S MOVE IN SILENCE

By **Von Diesel**

Nicholas Lock

GHOST MOB
Stilloan Robinson
MOB TIES I II III IV V VI
SOUL OF A HUSTLER, HEART OF A KILLER I II III
GORILLAZ IN THE TRENCHES I II III
THE BLACK DIAMOND CARTEL
By SayNoMore
BODYMORE MURDERLAND I II III
THE BIRTH OF A GANGSTER I II III
By Delmont Player
FOR THE LOVE OF A BOSS
By C. D. Blue
MOBBED UP I II III IV
THE BRICK MAN I II III IV V
THE COCAINE PRINCESS I II III IV V VI VII VIII IX X
SUPER GREMLIN
By King Rio
KILLA KOUNTY I II III IV
By Khufu
MONEY GAME I II
By Smoove Dolla
A GANGSTA'S KARMA I II III
By FLAME
KING OF THE TRENCHES I II III
by **GHOST & TRANAY ADAMS**
QUEEN OF THE ZOO I II
By **Black Migo**

194

Confessions of a Jackboy 3

GRIMEY WAYS I II III

By Ray Vinci

XMAS WITH AN ATL SHOOTER

By Ca$h & Destiny Skai

KING KILLA

By Vincent "Vitto" Holloway

BETRAYAL OF A THUG I II

By Fre$h

THE MURDER QUEENS I II III

By Michael Gallon

TREAL LOVE

By Le'Monica Jackson

FOR THE LOVE OF BLOOD I II III

By Jamel Mitchell

HOOD CONSIGLIERE I II

By Keese

PROTÉGÉ OF A LEGEND I II III

LOVE IN THE TRENCHES

By Corey Robinson

BORN IN THE GRAVE I II III

By Self Made Tay

MOAN IN MY MOUTH

SANCTIFIED AND HORNY

By XTASY

TORN BETWEEN A GANGSTER AND A GENTLEMAN

By J-BLUNT & Miss Kim

LOYALTY IS EVERYTHING I II

195

Nicholas Lock

Molotti

HERE TODAY GONE TOMORROW

By Fly Rock

PILLOW PRINCESS

By S. Hawkins

NAÏVE TO THE STREETS

WOMEN LIE MEN LIE I II III

GIRLS FALL LIKE DOMINOS

STACK BEFORE YOU SPURLGE

FIFTY SHADES OF SNOW I II III

By A. Roy Milligan

SALUTE MY SAVAGERY I II

By Fumiya Payne

BOOKS BY LDP'S CEO, CA$H

TRUST IN NO MAN

TRUST IN NO MAN 2

TRUST IN NO MAN 3

BONDED BY BLOOD

SHORTY GOT A THUG

THUGS CRY

THUGS CRY 2

THUGS CRY 3

TRUST NO BITCH

TRUST NO BITCH 2

TRUST NO BITCH 3

TIL MY CASKET DROPS

RESTRAINING ORDER

RESTRAINING ORDER 2

IN LOVE WITH A CONVICT

LIFE OF A HOOD STAR

XMAS WITH AN ATL SHOOTER

Nicholas Lock